Tales from the Tide

Tales from the Tide

Contents

Acknowledgements 6
Introduction 7
Winners 11
   The Weight of the Wait *by Helen Murray* 12
   Ruby *by Jana Bakunina* 19
   Blue Sings *by Mary Ellen Fox* 24
Shortlisted... 34
   Albert *by Helen Bromovsky*................................. 35
   Fish Guts *by Natalie Hart* 45
   In Your Element *by Zelda C. Thorne* 54
   Mermaid *by Terry Davids* 60
   The Coastal Path *by Robert Stevens* 69
   The Man, the Boy and the Sea *by Charlie Robinson*... 78
   The Sea *by Fran Pridham* 88

Tales from the Tide

Anne Funnell Members' Shield 97
   Breaking Through *by Samantha Mattocks* 98
   The Once Golden Sea *by Iain Andrews* 106
   The Eye of the Storm *by Simon Conner* 115
   Soul to the Sea *by Christie Davies* 125
   The Wedding of the Sea *by Michael Giddings* .. 135
Author Biographies 144
A Tribute to Olga Sinclair 155
About the Norwich Writers' Circle 158

Compiled and edited by Iain Andrews. Cover illustration by Kathy Joy.

All stories are the copyright of their respective owners and are used here with their permission.

No part of this publication may be reproduced, distributed, or transmitted in any form or by any means, including but not limited to photocopying, recording, or other electronic or mechanical methods, without the prior written permission of the publisher, except in the case of brief quotations embodied in critical reviews and certain other non-commercial uses permitted by copyright law.

The stories featured in this anthology are works of fiction. Names, characters, businesses, events and incidents are the products of the author's imagination. Any resemblance to actual persons, living or dead, or actual events is purely coincidental.

Acknowledgements

The Norwich Writers' Circle would like to thank our adjudicators, Dr Susan Burton and Jo Wilde, for their hard work judging the stories.

We'd also like to thank everyone who entered, and those who have continued to support us by sharing the competition on their social media and with friends and family. It means the world to us to be part of such a supportive community.

Introduction
By Main Story Adjudicator Dr Susan Burton

The theme, the sea, has many possibilities. It is a liminal space, between known and unknown, safety and danger, life and death. Entries included stories of:
- Fantastical: mermaids and selkies, ghosts, talking fish.
- Historical: fishing industry, shipwrecks, wartime.
- Ecological themes: several set in Norfolk and dealing with flooding and coastal erosion.
- Sci-fi: including apocalyptic/end of days stories. Also combining sci-fi and ecological such as John Wyndham-esque stories which mix the domestic with the fantastical.

Although the stories are about one key incident, the best relate to a wider theme including: Catholicism, homosexuality, death, suicide, fishing as a dangerous industry, ecology issues and anti-capitalism.

Tales from the Tide

There were 123 entries. I read them all twice. It was relatively easy to reach a long longlist of 23 stories which I believe are publishable with or without further editing. Deciding the longlist of ten was harder but first place was a no brainer. I read about ten a day. That had an impact on judging because a good short story has to grab your attention immediately when you're reading so many.

Judging Criteria

I was probably quite technical at first reading - having sat through enough writing workshops at the UEA.
- Title: does it capture the story to follow.
- First sentence: does it grab the reader's attention - does it set up the story to follow.
- Dialogue: is it realistic and natural for the piece. Clean with no waffle.

My keyword was IMMEDIACY: the reader has to be in the moment from the get go.

Characterisation: we must know our protagonist from the get go, perhaps by their first action or the first words they say, or first thing we learn about them. Examples from the entries include: a boy who doesn't own any shoes, a story that starts with a sentence spoken by a man who covers his mouth and talks in a faint voice, and a man who fumbles with the buttons of his phone.

Connected to that is emotion: either building to that emotion, or else conveying a strong emotion from the get go. Dropping your protagonist into the thick of the action immediately connects them to the reader through that emotion, as the reader immediately understands there's something at stake.

No matter how fantastical it might be - is the story believable. I read technically but the best short stories made me forget that. When I found myself reading to find out what happens - when I believed it - when I was in the moment - I realised I had a potential winning short story.

I was not looking for 'uncooked' stories, e.g. unedited. With too many words: adverbs and adjectives, too much description, too many characters. 2,000 words is short, so every word counts.

I was not looking for stories in which the first paragraph was solely description, either of place or of the weather. The reader knows what a beach looks like, and what a storm feels like. Rather than beginning with an information dump, the best stories wove description into the story. Some stories could have been hugely improved by cutting out the first paragraph - or more - and beginning where the action starts.

Tales from the Tide

A worrying amount of stories were about women going to the sea to remember dead husbands - with or without their ashes! But memories, flashbacks and backstory meant that some stories lost their immediacy, and often meant that the protagonist in a short story was simply standing on the beach. The best short stories imply action from the word go.

Winners

1st Place
The Weight of the Wait
by Helen Murray

He never knocks, just comes right in.

'Shut the door behind you, Dad, it will bang.'

Too late. Salty wind blows through and the washing I've carefully pegged out behind me whirls about and catches in my hair. The wooden stool that I've been using as a doorstop starts sliding back over the cobbles and I've just time to grab the bowl of water carefully balanced atop before the stool tips to the ground and the door slams. Cold seawater splashes down my apron and, in doing so, the crab I've been scrubbing almost escapes on a tidal wave.

Through the back window, I catch sight of the old man. He rolls up the sleeves of his worn blue woollen gansey revealing his brown arms, turned to leather by the salt and sun. He uses the boot jack to lever out a foot and as he does so, dried herring scales and sand fall out of his knee-high sea boots.

Placing the crab in the crate alongside the hundred others from yesterday's late haul, I rub my sore hands against my sides before joining him in the kitchen. I see my father look in silent appraisal at the oilskins and wet slops that lay over a hangar by the fire. His daughter has made a good fishwife.

'Cup of something warm, Dad?'

'Sprat' he begins. His pet name for me, his baby herring. After four girls, I was supposed to be the much longed for boy. A son to go on the boats. When the local goodwife broke the news, the story goes that he came in and took me from mother. Worn from childbearing, he knew there would be no more. 'Some things are not meant to be, little Sprat,' he had said and passed me back.

There is a look of urgency in my father's rheumy eyes. His breathing is quick and shallow.

'Are Jack and Gilly ashore?'

My heart beats a little quicker. I've been trying to ignore the overcooked stew I've had on the go for my husband and my boy. I like to have a hot meal ready for them when they come off the boats. The clock on the church tower for lunch chimed a full hour ago.

'No, Dad. Not yet.'

'I found some of the lads waiting in the lookout to help bring them in over the swell when they come in. They sent me up to you to check whether they'd made land elsewhere and maybe walked home. Just had word old Whiskers Harrison stopped at Runton. Wind is blowing a good un. Rest of the boats are in, turned for home. Should we not go to shore, Sprat? Watch for the boys? Gilly will be cold and wanting his Mum, I'm sure.'

My Gilly. Only fifteen. Choking bile rises in my throat.

We had woken this morning, if you can call it that, in the darkest hour of the night. As I brewed the breakfast tea, Jack checked the glass. It was low so there was a discussion, but a catch must be caught and a living made. He made the decision to go out. All the fishermen did. The storms do whip up the crabs. They all know the bigger the risk, the greater the haul. As I watched him gulp down his tea, I wanted to tell Jack to leave Gilly in his bed. The knot in my stomach twisted causing a swell of nausea. My tea was set aside unfinished. Of course, Gilly was not the only son going out with his father and when I had clocked 'old Red' and his son, James – who had not inherited his father's copper hair – stroll past our door looking unconcerned, I had roused the lad.

A fizzing bang fills the air. Father rushes out and looks to the sky. 'It's a maroon. Got to get to the lifeboat. It's got to be for our Jack and Gilly.' Another bang splits through the howling wind. Struggling back on with his boots, he rushes out heading right to the gangway. On the other side of our narrow street, Mrs

The Weight of the Wait

Francis appears, flour in her hair. Behind her rushes out Jimmy, baggy eyed and harassed. I've seen Jack do the same. When one is in trouble, they all come running.

A third and final maroon.

All us women have their turn. Eventually. I've watched others suffer. Faces etched with anxiety. The relief when the men come in, and the horror when they don't. My coat is on before I shut the door. As I cut through the churchyard, billowing black clouds hover threateningly above. There is no choice but to pass the resting place of 'Old Billy,' everyone in Cromer knew him. Etched upon the stone is his foundering boat, a persistent reminder of the men the sea has taken. For all his tales of the dangers of longshore fishing, it was a simple swell that took him. Boat capsized as he passed the breakwater. Seaboots filled and down he went. One of the lads on shore told a ghastly tale of Old Billy's mouth turn into a horrible black circle before he went down and never came back up. Please God, don't take my boys today.

The gangway is heaving. Having seen and heard the maroons, towns folk have dropped their occupations and hurried to the shore, eager for the best spot to watch the boat launch. Pushing through the throng, I get to the railings and look over to the choppy sea, desperate to see the prow of The Marie come over the swell. They are nowhere in sight.

'Breaks up a gloomy Friday, if nothing else' says a grubby looking housewife next to me. There's lipstick smeared on her snaggly teeth. In her hands she twists a dirty green cloth. She must have run out mid dusting. 'Give that to me' I snatch it from her hands and throw it over the wall into the stormy waves below. 'You should know green is unlucky!' She looks at me, half angered and half bemused.

I start for home. I cannot be out here. Watching. Waiting. I let myself back in and gently rearrange the slops on the airer. The kettle is only half full. I shall get it on. For the boys. Removing the cloth covering the stew, I stir with a spoon and touch it to my lips. It's still warm.

Interminable minutes. One or two locals pass my window on their way back home, bored after the boat launch, or just too cold to hang around. The wind screams down the chimney pot.

The crabs and lobsters still need to be dealt with. Ain't going to sort themselves. Back out in the yard. Gilly's woolly gansey whips at me. Jack's broom falls from the wall. I set the water to boil slowly and gently add in the crabs. The shock of being submerged in boiling water makes them shed their claws so it must

The Weight of the Wait

be done slowly. Do they feel panic, or pain? I had never thought of it before.

My stomach heaves and vomit splashes by my feet. I can't move, can't breathe.

The church clock strikes.

'Ma?'

It can't be.

I hear it again. 'Ma?' followed by a muffled 'Dad, she's not here.'

'Must be by the gangway, son. She will be worried sick. Go down to the shore lad. Let the boys know.'

It's Jack. I can do nothing but run to his arms, trembling.

'Come to, mother. Tis ok now.' He strokes my hair. 'Gilly is safe, I've sent him off to the gangway to let them know. We had to come off at Overstrand. I couldn't risk the boy.'

I am in his arms where there is nothing but a spreading warmth. A minute passes where everything is right in the world. I break loose to get myself together and I use the end of my apron to dab my eyes. 'No matter, no matter. Stew is ready.'

Shortly after, Gilly arrives home. With him are some of the lifeboat men. Jack shakes each hand in turn, and I hear murmurs of thanks. Waiting for them to leave, I'm by the fire ready to strip off their wet things. Ready for tomorrow and another wait.

Tales from the Tide

Feedback

This story has it all: it begins in the thick of the action with a door banging open and the announcement of a potential tragedy: a fishing boat has failed to return. This raises fear and a sense of dread in both the protagonist and the reader from the start. The dialogue is detailed and authentic while descriptions of the fishing life are seamlessly woven into the fabric of the story from the 'maroon' flares which summon the lifeboat crew to the way in which the wife rearranges the slops on the airer to distract her from the absence of her husband and son. The story is dense with historical detail. Specialist words - gansey and spats - help to place the reader in a time as well as a place. The characterisation is strong. We know the wife through her attempts to stave off nausea through calming actions such as making the tea but we are also aware of the panic that threatens to overcome her when she tosses away an unlucky green cloth. The happy ending - at least for one day - is vital. It rewards the reader for the emotional ride they'd been taken on. As soon as began reading, I knew this was the winning story.

2nd Place
Ruby
by Jana Bakunina

"What if Sarah is right?" You said that sitting on a sofa with your chin pointing up towards the ceiling. Your hand was covering your mouth, so I could barely make out your voice. Then again, Sarah goes on about one thing only: she wants us to move closer to Cambridge. She's been looking at new developments in the area. She doesn't trust us on our own anymore.

I went to the kitchen for some water.

It was a hot afternoon. We went to the beer garden, where you like to nurse half a pint on a Sunday. A drop of blood landed on your trousers. Your nose was bleeding. What were you thinking going out in the sun without a hat? We rushed home. Our old house stays pleasantly cool during the day. It was a welcome retreat.

You lowered your head and dabbed at your nose. The napkin was dry. You noticed me sulking.

"I didn't mean that, Ruby", you said, getting up from the sofa. I didn't move and closed my eyes. I knew it wasn't just about the nosebleed.

In the morning, we went for a walk along the coastal path a little later than usual. You woke up feeling stiff in your joints. It took you a second cup of tea to get going. On the way back, we went down to the beach. In summer, Cornwall gets crammed with families coming to the seaside. My eyes are weak, but I could tell the beach was busy from the smell of the sun cream slapped on sun worshippers and hearing the children squeal in delight. Amidst the joyous kerfuffle and blinded by the sun, I became disoriented and lost sight of you. I wish I had that surgery to remove cataracts from my eyes, but I'd managed quite all right until today. I came up to a man wearing the same hiking boots as you, but he smelled of tobacco. I kept looking, navigating toddlers and sandcastles, until you caught up with me. You teased me about it on the way home.

"Shall we have some supper?"

We don't cook much. I have my usual. You heat up a tin of three beans soup. You've never been much of a meat eater. But you have a sweet tooth, while I don't. I like cheese though, on occasion. We aren't fussy: there is a cupboard full of boxes and tins, all neatly stored. After supper, we watch TV on the sofa until we

Ruby

doze off. We've had the same routine ever since I moved in with you some ten years ago. I was young then. They say infants cannot survive if deprived of touch. I can't imagine life without snuggling up to you either.

Sarah calls to remind us they are coming on Thursday. You are too savvy to tell her about me getting disoriented or the afternoon accident. You complain about the crossword you've been trying to tackle all weekend, mocking me. "Ruby isn't much help!" Neither is Sarah, mind. She only calls to fuss.

I never had children myself. Sarah, I know, means well, but it's always the same. With your hearing going, you put her on the phone's loudspeaker: "Dad, I know it's hard to persuade you to leave Cornwall, but I worry about you. If anything happens..." Whenever they come over, it feels like an inspection. "Have you been taking those supplements I got you? It's calcium and vitamin D." When she thinks I'm not looking, she opens the fridge and the cupboards to check if we remembered to stock them.

"You lead such a reclusive life. In Cambridge, there are museums and art galleries, and community clubs with yoga classes for the elderly." Don't make me laugh.

The next morning, we set off early. It's my favourite time of the day. They say the old are invisible, but it's only because the young are always rushing. We take our time. The beach is empty, but the birds were here earlier. Back up the path, the grass is heavy with dew. We say hello to Abigail and her Scottish terrier, Archie. Abigail had her hip replaced last year. She is flying now – Archie can barely keep up with her. We get to our favourite place, a bench that looks out over the bay. The air smells of salty weed. We rest there in the calming presence of the sea. Our small world expands all the way to the horizon. "No art gallery can replace this", you say. We walk back in silence, interrupted only by restless seagulls.

It's Thursday. You are in charge of hoovering. We picked some wildflowers in the morning and put them in jam jars. We have fresh milk and butter in the fridge, and a loaf of bread on the counter. You've even combed your hair and put on your good shirt. We hear a car on the gravel. I look you in the eyes. You hold my gaze, and you say: "We'll be all right, Ruby, you and me". You pat me. We hear the impatient footsteps on the gravel and the kids knocking on the door. They'll cause a ruckus for sure, but I don't mind. You get up, and I follow you to the front door to greet them. I'm wagging my tail. I even bark.

Ruby

Feedback

I didn't see that coming! This story is deceptively simple which is, of course, difficult to achieve. At first reading I found it well-written if a little humdrum - until I read the last two lines. That sent me back to the beginning to reread it with fresh eyes. And then I wondered how I didn't spot it. I didn't spot it because it is cleverly done. There were many entries about older people wandering the beach while considering issues of ageing and overbearing children. Some were a little depressing. But his story, despite touching on the same themes, has at its core a big heart, that of its caring - and surprising - protagonist.

3rd Place
Blue Sings
by Mary Ellen Fox

Many years ago, before I came to Tanganyika, sometime during the summer of 1947, there had been a famine. The brothers had been three days without food and when they looked up into the hills, they saw the topmost crag on fire and took this for a sign. They climbed the crag three leagues hence. As they neared the summit, they realised the glow was from a swarm of yellow honeybees, their wings agleam in the low afternoon sun. The empty beehive, brimming with honey, drew all manner of animals to it, thus providing plenty of meat for them to hunt and feast upon. A day was set aside for rejoicing and prayers, and the meat and honey were shared with the villagers. The sign had been a good one. And then came the day when I first set eyes on you Albi and you were my sign.

I remember that evening well. There was no wind. On the beaches around Stonetown, the turtles were laying their eggs. The moon was a coin hanging low in a black sky and I could see you clearly. Just out to sea, away from the sand near some rocks, you lay on your back and some seaweed had attached itself to your hair so that strands of it floated behind you. You were naked and your skin glowed white and your hair was whiter still. For a moment, I thought you were an angel with the seaweed strewn out behind you in silver streaks. You floated like this until the water spun you slowly round and your foot caught in a rock cleft.

And then the brothers appeared from behind the rocks as though the rocks themselves had come to life. They lifted you and they covered you with an old sail from their fishing boat and brought you to me. And your eyelids fluttered like the most delicate white moths.

Brother Peter laid you down on the floor. And you stayed in my room for the next three weeks. I watched you. Apart from the angry scab below your right shoulder blade and a gash on your forehead, your flesh was so white and perfect that I was almost compelled to reach out and touch you to make sure you were real.

*

When I awoke one morning, you were watching me.

'Good morning, Sir. I was just making you some tea.' Your Swahili was perfect.

I raised myself up onto one arm. 'Aaaah. So, you speak.' I felt my face flush. 'Are you feeling better?'

'Much better, sir. Thank you. You have looked after me very well. And the cut is nearly healed.'

'Yes, nearly healed. But still quite red. So, you will need to keep an eye on it. So, tell me. How on earth did you end up here?'

'I am sorry sir. I don't have much memory of what happened. Only that I was being chased and I climbed into a fishing boat to hide and it must have drifted out to sea.'

'What about your mother and father?' You shook your head.

'My mother is still at home in our village, but my father died before I was born. I am sorry but I don't remember much' You would not look me in the eye, and I felt sure you were not telling me the whole story.

'Never mind. Give it time and your memory will return. Your village; where is it on the mainland?'

'It is called Nmumba, about five miles from the coast.'

'So, do you have a name?' You shrugged but said nothing. I took this as a sign that you could not remember.

'Your skin and hair are most strikingly white. You are albino. Did you know that?'

'Yes Sir. My mother told me.'

The Blue Sings

'So, until you remember your real name, may I call you Albi?'

You stared at me for a moment and then your face cracked into a startling wide grin. 'Albi. Yes Sir. I like that.'

You walked over to the table. 'You are an artist?'

I realised I had left my latest illumination stretched open. I had grown tired of it and hadn't touched it in weeks.

'Ah yes. My main work here is as a missionary, but I was also called here to illuminate this book. The Gospel of St Mathew. I really should start work on it again.'

You drew a long elegant finger over the capital seraph. 'It is beautiful. Such rich colours.'

'Thank you. I'm glad you like it.'

'Where do the pigments come from?' You had to bend over so you were close to the page and I realised your eyesight was poor.

'The green comes from Verdigris collected from copper in Crete. The copper sheet is left in the rain and it oxidises and……'

'Yes sir. I know. My mother has told me how Verdigris is made.'

'Of course. And the blue is crushed lapis lazuli all the way from Kabul.'

'So, merchants pass through here?'

'Well no. I have gathered the pigments on my travels actually. Before I was a priest, I travelled round with the merchant navy and so I picked up the pigments wherever I could find them. Old artist shops. Markets. That sort of thing.'

'And before that?'

'Ah before that. I studied Classics at Cambridge.'

Your eyes opened wide.

'In England? Oh, I would love to go there. And now you have a new queen.'

'Yes. We do. How on earth did you know that?' I put up my palm to stop him speaking. 'Don't tell me. Your mother told you?'

He laughed at this.

'How wonderful the world is. And I know so little of it.'

'I can teach you more about the world Albi. If you will let me?'

You gave me an even look and tilted your head to the right slightly as though you felt you were being tested somehow.

'Ultima tentatio Christi.' He read the words slowly, 'what does that mean?'

'It means "The Last Temptation of Christ."'

'So, who is Christ and who is tempting him?'

The Blue Sings

'My goodness – You are full of questions and yet you have no answers.' You said nothing to that, and I feared I had offended you.

'It needs more blue. Here. And here. And a drawing here. Of the temptations. I love the blue. The blue sings.' I looked at you with complete astonishment because you were so right. I sat down on the bed and laughed. I could not help myself.

And so, the days passed. All the brothers liked having you here and gave you special jobs to do, apart from Brother Peter who simply watched you. I would work on my illumination, sharpening the colours and adding more blue and day by day it became increasingly more beautiful to me.

Your main task involved tending the two sows in the barn. I often stole down to talk to you. You would ask me questions about the Church, my travels, all manner of things and I would answer you as best I could. I often brought you down spiced chai and ugali with warm chapattis as I thought you might have been hungry but really, I just wanted to see you.

'So, your village elder chased you down to the shore because you let the boars escape?'

'Yes.' You turned away and stirred the glass of coffee.

'Is that true Albi or did something else happen?' He stared at his glass for a long time.

'It was not the village elder but some men.'
'What men?'
'I do not know but they wanted my white flesh or that is what my mother told me. She helped me escape.'
'So, they wanted to kill you because you are albino?'
'Yes. Many children die this way.'
'I see.'
'I am so sorry Albi. You should not have to hide and run for your life.' I touched your pale fingers, and you let me.
'I will stay here tonight. I want to be on my own.' So, I left you to make a bed in the straw.

*

Just a few days later on the evening before you left, you were down by the shore with Brother Peter. You were catching mackerel with a swiss army knife. There was a flash of silver in the green seaweed as something whipped around. You started quickly towards it; blade held out at arm's length. 'Snake, snake! 'I heard Brother Peter cry. The black thing whipped around to strike. I was so frightened. Paralysed with the shock with just my fists opening and closing. You jabbed at the serpent and the with a stifled cry you managed to pin the back of its head to a rock.

The Blue Sings

You came to my bedchamber that night and climbed into my bed. You did not say anything, but your shoulders were stiff. I had a balm of mint and flax oil which I sometimes used to soothe the brother's feet. You turned your back to me, and I could smell burnt charcoal on you. There were even tiny flecks of dead embers in your hair. I lifted myself onto an elbow and poured the balm into my hand. I lifted your hair gently clear of your nape. As I rubbed the salve into your shoulder, I noticed how old and grubby my own hands appeared: the nails black and the fingers bent out of shape. If I moved to one side, I could just make out the fluttering of your half-closed eyes, the curve of your neck. I thought you were asleep so this time I rubbed in the ointment as quickly as I could with my eyes shut. I felt very hot and a little sick in my stomach. I felt suddenly unmoored. Adrift. Undone. I desperately wanted you to stay. But I knew I could not keep you.

'I can't stay here.' You were awake after all.

'You can Albi. We will find a room for you.'

'No. I can't. I must move on. Brother Peter does not trust me.'

'Where will you go?'

'I don't know. I will steal away in a ship from Dar and travel round the world. Like you used to. Perhaps to England where the people are as white as me. And

I will visit our new queen.' He flashed his startlingly bright grin.

'If I write you a letter, will you answer it?' I whispered.

'My writing is not so good. Not nearly as good as yours.'

'But would you try? It does not matter about the writing. Just to tell me what you are doing?'

'I would have nothing to say. It would be very dull.' He smiled at me.

'So, you're saying yes then to a letter? Please. Please say yes. I tried to drag an answer out of you.'

'Yes then. I will write when I can. If you send it to my village, it will find me.'

And that was the last time we were together. From the window I saw you walk down to the beach, naked as the day you arrived, ready to swim out to a little fishing boat where you had hidden some clothes, some food, some money. I watched you. A log. A lily adrift on the current. And just when I thought you were heading out to sea you flipped over and began to swim slowly but with deliberate strokes. Hugging the shore. You turned toward the window. One last look. My heart hammered. I watched you all the while. You took your time. You headed for the little boat that would take you to the ship that would take you to who-knows-where? Ephesus, Crete, Kandahar maybe? And

The Blue Sings

then you passed beyond the harbour wall and you were swallowed. Nothing to be seen but the eternal sea moving over its bed of stones. I knew this moment would come. I knew I could not keep you. Not forever. I was right about that.

Feedback

As soon as I began to read this, I got 'Graham Greene' vibes. The location? The subject matter? The Catholicism? Maybe all three and all three were excellently described and woven into the story. There were several contenders for third place but this story pipped the others due to its excellent dialogue, both explanatory (without detracting from the story) and the role it plays as the two protagonists learn about each other. A short story with a text and a subtext cleverly filtered through the thoughts of its first person narrator.

Tales from the Tide

Shortlisted

Albert
by Helen Bromovsky

Albertino grew up on the beach. A little beach with pebbles, tough on the feet, but not for a boy who had never owned a pair of shoes. In those days the islands were rarely visited. Only by an occasional yacht, a huge monster emerging from the sea.

Albertino's family had, it seemed, always lived on the island. The family grew and cultivated what they needed on the fertile land. At different times of the year and cycle of the moon they enjoyed the pleasure of some sort of abundance; juicy figs, ripe tomatoes, aromatic lemons, or sea delicacies in huge supply, and enduring little at other times. Grapes, vines, wine were carefully, lovingly distilled by the grandfather with his mesmerising rituals during the full moon, harvesting and cherishing to create his cup he called nectar, soaked in the balmy sea air. Occasionally shared with others and something that made him very happy, sometimes he would then kiss little Albertino on the forehead with passion.

Days passed, generally happily, except sometimes, when not much was to be had but dried seaweed.

Tales from the Tide

Never mind, the plenty soon returned, and it was feted. The family worked to the same end, growing, preparing, eating, following the cycles of sun and moon, drought, floods, gales and silence, abundance, and deprivation. A way of life.

Albertino and his brother were shown the magical mysteries of fishing and farming. His father was the fisherman and ventured out rain or shine in his tiny wooden tub. He quietly reappeared, often fish-less, sometimes brow-beaten or with a smile the width of the new moon when bearing a booty of fish. Never expected to work on the land or the fire, his place was the sea and the fish and the privilege of bearing the family with delights from the deep blue depths. One day the waves were high, the wind howled, and the swell crashed violently onto the pebbles. The father stoically and courageously launched his little wooden boat into the raging sea. He didn't return. Some time later as the full moon rose again the planks from the hull washed up on the beach. Soon after, Albertino's brother took the mantel, built a little wooden tub, and re- traced his father's footsteps hunting and providing for the family.

Nothing was said. Life went on. The duties, trials and tribulations of the family, the island, the hut, where they lived, the sea, the fertile pastures, the trees, the stony beach continued in harmony.

Albert

One fine day, the mirage where blue meets blue, the sea and the sky accompanied Albertino. He was stoking the fire for his mother to smoke the fish to a soft warm red glow, an idyllic hue and temperature for her to create the succulent flesh of her fresh fish dish, with garlic, parsley, sea salt and olive oil. His peace was interrupted by a roar arriving from within the blue mirage, a shiny white motorboat chugged in and threw anchor in front of the beach. A tanned man with dark glasses wandered onto the pebbled beach, grimacing, struggling to walk in his bare feet on the hard stones. Albertino jumped down from the fire, excited by a visitor. He ran down the slope to the water's edge, held out his hand for the visitor to find his balance, and hand-in-hand they climbed the beach.

Albertino welcomed the guest with jasmine tea, bread, and seaweed-infused oil. With great pleasure Arnold accepted. They shared a language, although different in tone "Albertino", said Arnold, "What if we make a restaurant here? I will provide whatever you need. and bring guests. We are only an hour by speedboat from the mainland. It will be the 'toast of the coast'!

Albertino rushed to his grandfather and mother and announced the idea. They didn't understand. They had, of course, never been to a restaurant. They knew only the island, the family, and the occasional guest, who always seemed to them ignorant. They understood bounteous and sparse times, lunar seasonal phases, the delicate balance, and handling of life. Arnold explained in detail how it would work. Boats would bring supplies. The dear grandfather could relax and enjoy his retirement sitting by the sea with the mother.

After many trips from the tanned man with dark glasses, Arnold and Albertino had become conspirators. The restaurant would be named Albert, after his father and they would honour the fisherman lost at sea. Albert would be so proud of his dear son. Finally, grandfather and the mother came to the beach hut, with a bottle of the precious nectar and popped the cork. Glasses were raised to Albert.

A legion of boats, supplies and people splashed onto the beach soon after. The tranquillity of the island disappeared. By the summer solstice, 'Albert' awaited the first guests. Albertino and Arnold stood on the pebbled beach, Arnold still unable to withstand the pain of the natural stones. As the summer and the sea flowed so did the guests, the fish, the wine. That quiet little hut and pebbled beach, turquoise water, wildflowers, the sanctuary for birds had become a lively epicentre for music, laughter, sunglasses, hats, loud voices, loud sounds, and endless supplies of everything from everywhere.

Albert

Many seasons, many solstices passed, grandfather and the mother sat under palm shade away from the hut; the platform that Arnold had had built for them, away from the restaurant and the kitchen. One late afternoon Albertino tore himself away from his duties, dragged a chair through the sand to join his dear grandfather and mother. He had seen little of them since the restaurant, not like the old days. The vision of them in the distance under the palm shade gave him peace. As he sat down the stillness overcame him. He slowly realised that they were not able to talk. They were unlike him, upright and energetic in his chair. Their faces were dark and lined. There was an unfresh odour in the still air. He stared at them in horror. Empty bottles were strewn around them. Dumbfounded. He realised they were drunk. Drunk. He hadn't noticed the state of his revered family. Immersed in Albert, he hadn't noticed the true state of those nearest and dearest.

A short time later grandfather didn't wake up when Albertino pushed open the door to his room. He saw a puffy pasty body of a person that had been his grandfather. His mother, brother and he buried the old man at sea. No fanfare. Just the vast loud splash of the corpse attached to a large stone chucked off the edge of the little wooden fishing boat. A feast for the fish. That evening as Albertino sat pensively, mournfully on the grey pebbles, eyes closed listening to the lapping of the waves his mother and brother swam out to sea and did not return.

Albertino in the tranquil way he had been raised and all he knew did not shout and scream. He went back to the restaurant that night. He carried on with his work, serving guests, gutting fish, wiping down tables, erasing evidence of a previous plate. Albertino carried on like this, day after day, as the moon followed the sun and waves slid across the pebbles, every day. He carried on as before, cooking. The fire had lost its magic without his mother, the flame didn't dance anymore. One evening Arnold called out, "Albertini". As he now called him, "Bring me a fish". Albertini, diminished, like the reflection of his image in the water. Lonely and lost, angry, alone, empty. The island had lost its meaning. There was no nectar. Albert had ruined their lives.

Albertino had lived with the sea, grown up with the sea, inhabited the sea, as the sea had inhabited him. He knew the fish in the sea, at great depth, in shallow waters, plankton, seaweed, seagrass, the species of fish and fauna. He had noticed sadly over time the diminishing presence of some and then the sudden presence of strange new species, particularly fish. The orange shiny, bright crazy fish, like the crazy music in the bar that had started to appear. He knew this intruder

Albert

would eat their indigenous fish. He knew, what he called the 'disco' fish was dangerous.

One evening, with the warm memory of his grandfather's nectar kiss within him he quietly pushed his brother's little wooden fishing boat onto the glistening surface of the sea. From the bow of the little boat with a fishing net on a stick he carefully caught one of the brightly coloured incongruous, un-indigenous 'disco' fish. He carefully, quietly took it to the kitchen, meticulously skinned it, as he knew how, and cut out slithers of the filet. He sliced the spines into tiny pieces, wherein he knew to be venomous, toxic. He put them carefully in a little bowl with a marinade of olive oil and nectar. In a corner in the refrigerator, he placed his filleted fish and small bowl camouflaged with lettuce leaves. He stepped outside the kitchen, dug a hole, and buried there the skin, bones, and evidence of the outlandish 'disco' fish. He tip-toed to bed.

As always Albertino rose early with the sun. Peacefully he brushed the floor of the restaurant, scrubbed the wooden tables, as the swell and wash clean the rough stones on the beach, as the sun follows the moon and light follows dark. He left, as always, the scene prepared and ready for the migration of the intruders, their guests at Albert. He went off to doze on his bed, as always, as the island workers mobilised themselves, like ants on a mound. "Albertini!" He woke with a start from his reverie, a dream of his father, mother, brother, and grandfather at peace at sea, floating joyfully in the turquoise depths. "Albertini! Where is my fish?" Bellowed Arnold invading the sanctuary of his sleepy ear and his imaginary idyll.

"So sorry, so sorry Arnold", he muttered as he righted himself and wandered sleepily to the kitchen. The shrine, that had been the domain of his dear mother, from where they had, in days gone by received with gratitude the delights and nourishment of land and sea. "It won't be long" and to himself he whispered, "Peace at last".

Albertino carefully removed his fish and small bowl from the refrigerator. He fried the fish over a blazing flame, prepared a green salad with the lettuce and tipped the marinated contents from the bowl into the garlic sauce with finely chopped parsley that he had created to embellish the dish. "It's coming Arnold", he called over. "The cycle of life continues", he whispered presenting the plate with exaggerated gusto and a wide 'new moon' smile spread across his lips towards his feckless friend. "Here it is". Arnold picked up his knife and fork, licked his lips, and shovelled the white fish submerged in the green sauce and shunted it enthusiastically into the mouth of his tanned face beneath the dark sunglasses.

Albert

Albertino watched quietly. One more shovel, and another. "So good, this life", muttered Arnold. Then, suddenly he lurched forward. His head and face collapsed into the plate. He stopped breathing instantly.

Albertino wandered back to the kitchen to bring a glass of water to the voracious diner. As he returned a small crowd had assembled. "Was he asleep?" One asked. There was a doctor on the adjacent table. "Goodness. No pulse." They called a motorboat and with remarkably little commotion whizzed him back to the mainland across the glistening sea. The guests continued eating their seaside lunch. Albertino brushed the floor again and scrubbed the tables.

He longed to return to his reverie; infused with the glowing red of the heat from the fire, the calm of the dark blue shades of the sea, the thrashing waves and the white drift crashing onto the grey pebbles, the nectar and the soft balmy feel of his grandfather's lips with that passionate loving kiss.

Tales from the Tide

Feedback

A culinary short story set on a fertile island with descriptive language that allows the reader to smell and taste the island's delicious produce, before the family's simple island life is despoiled by capitalism - an allegorical tale here, I think. Although of a slower pace than other stories in the competition, it suits the tale of island life and gradually builds to a satisfying denouement. While the title 'Albert' is perfectly serviceable, I wonder if there might be another which more fully describes the narrative. Maybe 'The Disco Fish'?

Fish Guts
by Natalie Hart

'Throw a stone into the sea on a Sunday and your hand will go with it.'

All the children wanted to see if it was true. None of them wanted to be the one to risk it. The English passages of the Bible they learned by rote were as murky as mist in the gloaming, but the Sabbath warnings in Gaelic from the minister were as clear as rock pools on a sunny day. The stakes of losing a limb were too high to take the chance on a stone. Being a fisherman or a fisherman's wife required both hands.

Jessie picked up a pebble from the shore. Its smooth form nestled perfectly in her palm. Throwing stones into the sea held no appeal to her during the weekdays, but on Sundays, the temptation was almost irresistible. She wanted to find out if it was true. But what if her hand did fly off into the waves never to be seen again? What if it didn't? What if she found out it wasn't true? What then? Would that mean she could do other things on the Sabbath? Would that mean the stern faced minister lied to them? Did that mean God lied to them? Would it mean there wasn't a God? Her faced flushed at the improperness of the thought, her spine tingled at the possibility.

She clutched the stone in her sweaty palm. She didn't throw it, but she didn't return it to the shore either. In the day she kept it in her pocket and at night tucked it under her pillow, dreaming of being brave enough to tempt God to make true on His threats. She clasped it whenever she burned to say something but knew she should keep her mouth shut. When the teacher beat her right hand with a belt for speaking Gaelic at school, she clutched it in her left. In church when the minister said, 'Let him that is among you without sin, cast the first stone', she rubbed her fingers on its smooth surface. If that were true, no one was a sinner around here, as they were more than ready to cast stones. They drove the Campbell family out for the sins of their forefathers at Glencoe. In the village you had one of half a dozen surnames or you were an incomer and weren't welcome. Jessie had the right surname and her family had lived there further back than anyone could remember. She knew she would grow up to do what generations of women before her had done. She'd marry one of the boys that she didn't slyly flirt with in church, spend her life covered in fish guts and swollen with babies. Men wanted a strong, healthy wife so she could carry him to his boat to keep his feet dry and who could walk for miles to sell their catch at market. They needed a wife with two hands to fix bait to the lines, clean and pack fish, and gut herring. Jessie fit the bill and by the time she came of age, she wasn't short of offers. No one understood why, one by one, she turned them down. Jessie wanted to say because pickings in the village were good for fish, but not for the sort of husband she wanted. The villagers would have told her that then she would die an old maid. Fishermen from either side of the firth took fish from the same sea, but they kept to their own women. Fisherwomen visited markets all along the coast, but they always went home to their own men.

Jessie was bone tired from the journey when she arrived at the market with a creel on her hip and a scarf wrapped around her long, brown hair. On a clear day, she could see this part of the coast from her doorstep. Sometimes rays of light broke through the clouds and illuminated the peaks and troughs of distant mountains, like an illustration of God's presence in the family Bible. Jessie didn't feel God in those moments. She felt the urge to wade into the waves, the ice cold water searing her skin until it was pleasantly numb and stay there until her teeth chattered.

The market is where she first met William. The sleeves of his thick aaron jumper pushed up above his elbows, revealing strong, sun weathered forearms. His eyes the colour of the sea on a stormy day and a pipe clamped in his full lips that quirked into a smile when he saw her. He was a fisherman from a village on the other side of that stretch of water.

At first, Jessie and William exchanged glances across dead fish, then they exchanged words, and finally, they exchanged vows.

She was happy with her choice of husband. He was handsome and kind, and most important of all, she hadn't grown up with him. She didn't know him as a snot faced 8-year-old pulling her hair in church or an arrogant 15-year-old bragging about how many fish he'd caught that day. He didn't remember the time she wet herself at church or fell into a rock pool face first. The locals expected her to move away, but the village was in Jessie's blood and William was happy to relocate. As a Highlander, a good protestant man and a strong fisherman he was no different to the locals. But they didn't see it that way. They had cast her friend Netty out for marrying a man two villages down. The villages practically ran into each other, but Jessie had to visit her by walking along the shore at night lest anyone see. The men never invited William to have a dram with them after a long day of fishing. They didn't invite the newlyweds to the ministers for tea after church. The children teased their beloved daughter

Fish Guts

Annie in the playground, telling her to swim back to where she came from. William was an incomer and always would be.

As the sun waned in the sky, Jessie scanned the sea with eyes such a pale blue that in candlelight, she looked like she had no irises at all. Looking for a glimpse of William's red boat, she clutched the stone in her fish splattered apron with calloused fingers and held Annie's chubby hand with the other. Some days, the sea was like a pond, only disturbed by the ripple of a seagull landing on it. Other days slate grey waves clashed against each other from every angle with the fury of Old Testament God. Seagulls taking off to avoid being smashed to bits in the boiling white surf. Wrecks that widowed women and left children fatherless haunted the village. No matter the weather, Jessie's grasp on the stone loosened when she saw William's boat reach the shore.

One day, the villagers might save enough money to build a harbour, but for now, the men helped each other bring their boats up from the sea. William had to drag his boat up alone. Watching him haul the vessel up the shore on his back, Jessie would clutch the pebble so hard in her palm that it hurt. His feet pushing against the shifting sands or balancing on stones that a high tide had unceremoniously dumped. When the waves brought in seaweed, she held her breath as he navigated the slippery and precarious surface. Once the boat was high enough to be safe from the tide, William would kiss Jessie's cheeks, ruddy from the sun and coarse with salt. He told her she was beautiful and didn't complain about the smell of fish she could never get out of her hair.

The day he lost his footing, and the heavy wooden boat crashed down on him, the stone fell from her hand and bounced on the dry dirt road. His back was broken. A merciful god would have let him die at that moment. But she had to hear his cries of pain for three days and nights wishing she could put him out of his misery like a fish gasping for air on the deck of a boat. Retrieving the discarded stone from the road, she held it to her forehead as she said hollow prayers to God and wailed desperate pleas to no one in particular. The doctor just shook his head, handed her some whisky, and laid a firm hand on her shoulder before leaving. Jessie didn't know if the whisky was for her or William.

The locals turned up for the funeral. Jessie bit her tongue and accepted the offers to help carry his casket from the very men who wouldn't help carry his boat. As was customary, the villagers stood outside their houses as they walked the coffin to the graveyard. She thought about throwing the stone on his coffin along with the dirt but she didn't. She was glad no-one came to the house after.

Fish Guts

Widowhood sagged her shoulders like creels of herring, but she was used to putting one weary foot in front of the other. Annie stayed with her grandmother when with an aching heart Jessie followed the herring from port to port. She had no choice if she wanted to keep a roof over their heads and food on the table. One evening, exhausted, Jessie slumped in front of the fire, enjoying the heat of the mesmeric flames licking the driftwood and contemplating the chores of the next day to the crackle of seaweed. There was a knock at the door. Frowning at the interruption she smoothed down her hair and answered. On her doorstep stood a man, cap in hand. A man who she had known her whole life. He had pulled her hair in church and copied her homework. She had turned him down at 17.

'Jessie Macdonald.' He said, using her maiden name. 'You've been on your own now for 2 years. Is it not time you took yourself another husband?'

Jessie trembled with anger and clutched the stone in her apron. She wanted to throw it, watch it hit him between the eyes and for him to crumple like Goliath.

'You'll come in and hang your coat on the nail behind his door, but you wouldn't help him carry his boat?' The words fired out of her mouth like shards of clam shells. 'Go away, and don't come back.'

Jessie slammed the door in his face before he could reply.

Tales from the Tide

On Sunday, she didn't walk the mile and a half inland to church. Instead, she hoiked up her skirts and took to the shore with her little girl in tow. They moved swiftly along the rocks. They both knew where to place their feet from hours of childhood play and the backbreaking work of collecting wilks. The coast curled around and once the village was out of sight, Jessie stopped. Pulling the oval grey stone out of her pocket, she ran her fingers along the stripe of orange that encircled it, like a painted egg at Easter. She turned it to watch the specks of silver sparkle in the sun. Her gaze drifted out at the sea, to the land across the water that gave her a husband and daughter. To the tides that always brought him home safe, only for him to die on land. She pulled back her arm.

'If you throw a stone on the Sabbath, your hand will go with it.' Annie said, chewing the end of her plait.

Jessie threw the stone with all her might. The swoosh of her blouse and her daughter's gasp sent it on its way, arching through the air. It hit the water, made a satisfying plop, and the waves swallowed it up. She wriggled the fingers of her now empty hand. It was still firmly attached to her wrist. She selected a stone from the shore, placed into her daughter's hand and smiled.

Fish Guts

Feedback

A well-paced story with an immersive location and a deeper meaning: the protagonist's rejection of her religious upbringing. The story is vividly descriptive particularly of the small, claustrophobic fishing village and the way in which its inhabitants display their prejudice against outsiders. The use of the stone to represent the protagonist's religious beliefs and her wish to challenge - and ultimately reject - them is nice symbolism. For this reason I would suggest strengthening the title by bringing in the stone.

In Your Element
by Zelda C. Thorne

In the hazy morning light, we walk down our cobblestone street towards the slumberous seafront, mother and daughter, moving as one. Pigeons brood in the rooftop rafters, huddled and content. I steal a glance at your profile as we turn the corner, eternally shocked — as mothers are — by how much you've changed.

When you were born, your father scooped you out of the inflatable bath set up in our living room, grinning as your tiny grey tail flapped at him.

"She's strong," he said, leaning over to place you on my chest, over my heart, "and she has your nose."

Joy pulsed through me as I heard you cry. Breathe. We didn't know if you would need air or water, being half-merfolk, but as it happened, either would have sufficed.

"How can you tell she's a girl?" I asked.

"Boys are born with white tails," he said. "The colouring comes later."

"Oh."

In Your Element

Spellbound, I gazed at your perfect head, eyes, ears, tuft of green hair — just like your father — and of course the tail.

"Hello," I said, drinking you in. "I'm your mummy."

Once you were in my life — our life — the years rushed by, unstoppable. Merciless. I worried as you mastered the transition from legs to tail, tail to legs, seemingly without effort.

Seemingly overnight.

Up ahead, a flock of seagulls swoop and dive, rushing wildly on the wind. You're a half-step in front of me now, pulled forwards by your very own current. Sand whispers underfoot as we edge down the side of the bay. Seaweed clings to the rocks. The surf roars.

"I wish Dad was here."

"Me too." I take your hand in mine and give it a squeeze. "He would be so proud."

We are in a small, private cove just south of the beach. The air is briny, heavy with salt.

"The weather's meant to be calm all week," you say, looking towards the horizon.

My stomach churns. You mean I shouldn't worry, that you'll be safe out there, in a world beyond reach.

"Can you hear them?" I ask.

A line forms between your eyebrows as you concentrate and my skin tingles; you look just like your father when you do that.

"Yes," you say, "they wait beyond the coral."

A chill wind blows around your head, the strands of hair lifting and swirling like ink spilled in water.

When you were a baby, we bought your first cuddly toy: a small, fluffy white penguin trimmed with silver. We named him Percy. You gurgled, mouthing his fur, pressing him to your chest as you slept. If I wanted to wash him, I had to sneak him away first thing in the morning so he'd be dry again at bedtime.

Foolishly, I tried to stop this moment from coming. Pointing out that I wouldn't be able to protect you, that you were too young to go alone, a child still. It worked for a while. But then one day I came home to find all your childhood toys and teddy bears shoved in black plastic bags, dumped outside by the bins. That afternoon, we faced off on the landing.

"You're not going," I'd said, putting my foot down. "We can talk about it another—"

"You can't stop me. I'm not a kid anymore."

"Please listen to me, you might not be a kid, but you'll always be my little—"

You slammed your bedroom door in my face so hard the floorboards shook. The hallway spun, forcing me to put one hand out to steady myself.

In Your Element

I wish I could do that now. You move into my arms, your head finding the soft spot of my shoulder. I fight back the tears, not wanting my vision to blur at this crucial moment.

"I love you, Mum."

I swallow; you're so impossibly beautiful. "I love you too."

I've done all I can to prepare you and it's time to let go. It isn't easy. I want to clasp your arms and hold you back, but I don't.

You remove your clothing, wade out a few paces and sit down. Waves lap at your stomach as you transform into the sea goddess you are. My hand covers my mouth.

Your blue tail has the chill sheen of frozen water: an iceberg splinter, broken off, floating away.

Finally, you swim out, your turquoise hair bobbing along, dipping in and out of the sapphirine liquid. Striated clouds of seafoam; a flash of glittering tail. You turn and wave, radiant, in your element. I wave back just as your tail slips beneath the surface.

I stand there for a long time, watching the waves roll, hoping for another glimpse of you. The sea rushes up the dusky sand and kisses my toes, as if in apology. Gold shimmers on water. With a sigh, I turn my back on the ocean.

You don't need me anymore.

Tales from the Tide

I return home in a daze. My keys clatter on the kitchen table, too loud. The house smells wrong. Your father would know what to do, what to say. If only he hadn't been a hero, saving those reckless teenagers from drowning out at sea. The storm tossing his body at the vicious, ragged cliffside. If only merpeople were immortal as I had always previously believed. I close my eyes; I shouldn't say the word 'if', it leaves a sour taste on my tongue.

Upstairs, I drift into your room. It is strange, distant, as if I'm looking at a photograph. Your lonely bed mourns sweet dreams and bedtime stories. Chin quivering, I pull back the duvet, slip inside and curl up like a shrimp, hugging my knees to my chest. I bury my face in your pillow, choking on my own tears. A hollowness gnaws inside of me.

It is as if you've died.

My hand trembles, sliding over the cool bed sheets and my fingers find something small and soft. Frowning, I pull it above the covers and my breath catches. It's Percy, your penguin. Not thrown out with the others then. He's still here, albeit secretly. His fluff has faded from the original snow-white to an almost grey. It doesn't matter. I'll hold Percy in your place, and I won't wash him. I grip him close, pressing him to my chest, over my heart.

In Your Element

And it feels like a promise.

Feedback

This is the perennial tale of the young flying the nest enhanced by the fact that, in this case, the daughter is a mermaid and feels the pull - not of university or a first job - but of the ocean. Beautifully described (I particularly liked the keys clattering on a table in the empty house) with the mother's memories seamlessly interwoven into the present action. A lovely story which brought a tear to my eye.

Mermaid
by Terry Davids

I sit by the stove. The wood is crackling merrily, a pan of soup on the top gently cooks, and behind, an urn of water warms.

The small cottage is cosy, I am crocheting more bright blankets to add to the colourful cushions and rugs strewn about the small room and adjacent bedroom.

The walls are rosy with firelight and the candles on the mantle waver gently in contrast to the wild whining dusk winds that howl around my small, low roof.

I'm warm and safe, as are my chickens and goat, safe within the adjacent stall, warmed by the chimney wall shared between us.

The storm off the sea, just a shore away twists in great waves of water and throws itself into the surrounding cliffs and cove.

Mermaid

Salty, my hound lies on the rag rug before the stove. Later, when I've stoked the fire with peat, he will follow me to my pillows and blankets and sleep on my bed.

But Salty pricks his ears and growls low. I hear nothing but the piteous cry of a gull, so close though? Something must have set it swooping from the cliff.

The dog is now wagging its tail and gives small coughing barks – the sort when there is someone at the door that he knows and likes.

I sigh, well, there's nothing for it but to open my small door to the full force and see who's there.

As I pull the door open a crack it flings wide as someone falls against it and into the room.

I begin to shake, what sorcery is this?

A milky white form falls onto the floor, and shockingly discloses the top half of a small pale girl as she flaps and flops on the floor. Not quite a tail, her legs are joined and from the pelvis down she is covered by a deep emerald tracery of forming scale. The sharp sea gull cries are issuing from her mouth as she struggles.

I start to drag her toward the fire, but she shudders and struggles and with my hands slippery wet from the holding of her I understand that she cannot come close to its flames.

She ends up leaning against the stone wall on a cover of sorts pulled from the settle.

Instinct made me tip some of the wash water warming on the stove into a cup, it was sea water and somehow, I felt this would be palatable for her.

She drinks gratefully, the keening sea gull crying ceases.

Salty came over slowly, sniffed her hand and then licked her.

Her face breaks into a smile, and I can see that Salty has warmed her heart.

"Can you speak?" I ask.

Her voice comes, husky and faint as a low wind.

"Yes, it's coming back to me…"

She stares down at her legs and this time there is a human sob rather than a gulls.

"I am turning and must return to the sea."

I sit back by the stove, and we speak, and indeed there was a tale of sorcery behind it all.

"I sang when the moon was on the waves," she whispers, "and it was then that I saw him."

She stares beyond me into the flames she could no longer go near.

"A great ship passed, full of light and laughter. He was on the deck watching the waves when his face found mine and I knew that we shared fire and passion and need.

I sang to him, and he murmured words of adoration."

Her beautiful eyes, now sea green now sea grey, turned in the firelight as they follow her mood.

"But the night passed," she mourns, "as did the vessel, and with dawn on the rim, it was moving into the harbour of a kingdom, his kingdom. We met in the sea caves deep beneath the cliffs his castle rose from.

They were long nights, that dazzled with love. He would lay on the rocks, his face close to the water and there, as my hands wound about his neck, we would share whispers and long, burning kisses…"

Tears fell.

I put more logs in the stove and watch the flames dip and flare across the small room.

"How did you end up like this?"

"Through not listening." She cries softly. "I looked to the old woman of the sea, the sea witch."

"What a pretty tale" the witch had goaded… "A tale of love my sweet, as foolish as they can come. But pay if you must… the price is always costly."

She stops with a gasp as she looks at her legs. I saw that; indeed, a beautiful emerald tracery was beginning to mesh across her legs.

Tales from the Tide

"Your tail is going to be very beautiful" I say, moved by the fear on her face.

The next day despite the salty wind and stinging rain, I set up a rough lean- to up against the stall. Closed on all sides, The front was open to the sea so she could look out across the steely waves. To finish, I wound a length of ships rope, rough and tarry, about a rock hunched beneath the sombre cliff face and pulled it across the shingle. Salty ran around me, barking into the wind, his tail waving furiously, but for me it was a hard trudge.

Her glorious, gull cry of pleasure when, after sliding her there on a blanket and helping her up onto the rock made it all seem worth it.

Over the time of her turning, I brought her shellfish and kelp.

I scoured the beach line when the tide was out, my old cold hands prising mussels from the wet rocks, hearing them plop into the water inside along with the kelp and small crabs I'd found.

She mewled with pleasure when I brought this to her, picking out each item daintily, biting into shells with her sharp pointed little teeth and gravely sucking out the sea water.

Mermaid

I brought her an old comb which she used on her moon pale hair. Each day her legs locked further into a glittering deep green tail and long, trailing fins.

We sat with her, Salty and me in the bitter afternoons until the cold drove us back to the fire.

Over these few days, her skin paled as the tail colour deepened, a light tracery of veins marbled her milk white skin.

Her odour too, altered from the scent of salty beach air to that of a deeper scent, like water in caves, deep and chillingly fresh...

She sang to us of cool depths where the rings of the Sun reflected in wave shadow.

She became more deeply entranced by the sea each day - and at night as I lay in my small warm cot, I could hear her, on the other side of the wall, keening and singing, like a wind blowing, like water running over gravel.

Salty loved her, he would sit by her for hours while she stroked his fur and crooned lovingly to him...

"He is gentle like a seal." She would say, her pale cold arms wrapped about his head. "But often he's too warm to touch for too long."

Tales from the Tide

We all know when the day comes. She is restless, her tail threshing in agitation.

"It will be dark when I leave." Her breath draws out long and deeply, it had adjusted to being deeper and longer as was needed in the depths…

The sea is still, the surf ghostly white.

The mermaid grows wild with both fear -and a terrible glittering joy.

Salty and I sit quietly by her side. marvelling in the fading light at what she had become.

She gleams, shining white, whilst her tail has become fabulously rich, jewelled, and iridescent, she trails veils of emerald fins.

The moon rises slowly into an icy night sky.

"You know how it will end." she breaths in her endless sea whisper.

I nod. "I know the tale."

Her cold hands reach out and hold my old, skinny ones and in long endless breaths sigh her thanks and goodbyes.

"Stay in the path of the moon," I suddenly beg "so that we can see you - so we can stay with you for as long as possible."

She mewls her promise and Salty and I then walk slowly beside her as with ungainly wriggling, she pulls her way across the sand and into its restless edge where the sea hisses along the shingle.

Mermaid

We watch as she struggles through the shallows and plunges into the glide and grace of deeper waters. She turns and waves and sends a fierce scream of joy back over the moon lit waves as she dips and dives.

For true to her promise, she stays in the moons path…

We stay, Salty and I quietly, sadly standing at the sea's edge.

She is pale now, as she now swoons back, all movement lost, as she floats on the shining ripples.

The moon is intensely bright.

We watch as her disintegration spreads out, a cloud of pearls as multitudinous as the stars in the deep night above.

"All for love" I weep softly.

But then we see… We are not watching a dying, suddenly we are watching a fusion as the Moon fills the spaces between her with its passionate light.

And she becomes gathered up and rises like a cloud…

Tales from the Tide

Feedback

In this competition there were several stories featuring mermaids. This one stood out because of the way in which the human woman changed into a mermaid. This was highly descriptive, beautiful and at times frightening. The story seems historical, it is certainly timeless. The dialogue is sparing and gives us just enough information. Our imaginations do the rest. Does the mermaid die at the end? This was not clear to me and I wanted to know - but this doesn't detract from the story.

The Coastal Path
by Robert Stevens

Old Dave, as the locals called him, who lived these last many years in a solitary salt-sprayed hut on the coastal path to Steephill Cove, was on his morning perambulation with Angus - a West Highland Terrier - when he noticed, reflecting in the sunlight, a thin, oily sheen lacquered across the sand. Leading Angus down to the horseshoe bay for a closer look, he discovered a strange reddish-brown tinge to the swell that was washing up on the shore. *Most unusual*, he muttered to himself. He couldn't understand why the water looked so cloudy and dense, but the air was cold and his lungs tight, so he moved on.

Back at the cove that evening, when Angus let loose and ran up and down the length of the beach disturbing the water's edge, a faint bluish-green luminescent glow appeared in the spray. *I've never seen anything like it, not in all my years walkin' him down there*, Old Dave said to the other drinkers in the Spyglass Inn that night. *Bloody remarkable, it was,* the old man mumbled as he pawed at his pocket and pulled out a phone. Turning it on, he fumbled with the plastic buttons, clicked them a few times then pressed it to his ear. *Still no luck?* the barmaid asked a moment later. *Not tonight, Shelly,* Old Dave replied before switching the thing off again.

The following morning, the wind blew a storm into Steephill Cove, and this time Old Dave wasn't the only one walking by the beach. As the waves crashed in, the couple who owned the sole building in the bay - the seasonal, sea-beaten *Crab Cottage* restaurant - were dragging their boat in from the squall when they stopped in the howling wind and stared. The lacquer from yesterday now covered the shore, but it was inches thick and layered with thousands of tiny sea creatures. The wings of sand hoppers and shells of spotted cowrie were mixed in with the bulging black eyes of pale cuttlefish and short spines of cushion stars. It was a thick, lifeless blanket that smothered the sand. *Well, that ain't right*, Old Dave proclaimed to the couple standing next to him, shaking his head and coughing. *We're supposed to have a party of ten coming for lunch today*, the couple bemoaned to each other, *call someone, darling, we need this cleared up before then.*

The local council didn't arrive that day. When they did come down to assess the scene the next morning, there was already a small crowd of people looking out across the cove. The crumbling, knee-high sandstone

The Coastal Path

wall that drew a line between the pebble pathway and the beach's edge was spilling over with fish. All the way to the breaking of the waves, sliding in and out with the water like coins in a penny pusher, fish were piled high atop the previous day's blanket. Slick mackerel, olive-green bass, and orange-spotted gurnard. Black-blotched plaice, mottled dover sole, and diamond-shaped brill. All of them staring blankly, marble-eyed, and dead in the morning air.

The council cordoned off the beach and put up signs. Old Dave tried to take some of the fish home for supper but *these might be poisoned*, said the local council types, *could be because of a plankton bloom. Nothing to do but remove them and incinerate the lot.*

By nightfall, half the fish had been cleared, but with the only access to the cove being via the coastal path due to the storm, the process was slow and laborious. *Bloody waste is what it is*, Old Dave muttered in the Spyglass that night, before pressing the phone to his ear again, shaking his head and switching it off once more.

When Old Dave picked his way past the cordon the next morning, teams of people were setting up a marquee outside *Crab Cottage*. In front of them was a line of grey seals, each one straddling the sandstone wall and leaning face first into the shingle of the path. There were thirty of them, their long, whiskered muzzles and wide-set eyes tilted sideways as if they had one ear to the ground. The silver-grey, coarse fur of their coats looked dried out and weary in the sun.

No visitors, old-timer, didn't you see the signs?, Old Dave was told as he was ushered away. *What the bloody hell is goin' on?* appealed the old man, trying to keep his footing on frail legs. *Not for me to say, fella. All I know is, it ain't oil. But all these dead animals, the whole place is probably hazardous.*

That afternoon, Old Dave joined the crowds that were forming at the top of the cliff edges overlooking Steephill Cove. It was quite a distance to the bay, and the storm had returned, blustery and brash, but the onlookers weren't deterred. No one paid any attention to the old man as they pushed past him to watch a local TV crew set themselves up inches from the edge.

The next morning, the sound of repetitive thumping from a helicopter's blades roused Old Dave from his sleep. After he had slowly climbed out of bed, he poured a tin mug of tea from the stove and noticed two people standing outside his porch. He couldn't remember the last time he had had visitors. *Can I help you two?* he asked, wrapping the cords of his dressing gown tightly around his weary, weathered skin. *Sorry, we didn't think anyone still lived here… We were up on the cliff top and were just trying to find a bit of shelter out of the storm. Have you seen what's happening in the bay?* Old Dave sipped his tea and scratched a patch of silver-grey hair on his sun-spotted head. *Oh yes, those poor seals, and the fish, most peculiar the 'ole thing...* The young man of the couple frowned at the word 'fish'. *Forget the fish*, he said, *there's some fuckin' killer whales down there!*

Once dressed, Old Dave walked Angus to the cordon and the unique patterned black and white splendour of four orcas was clear to see. *Jesus aitch*, he whistled, feeling the pain in his bulbous knuckles as Angus began barking and pulling on his lead. *When did they turn up?* he asked the guard. *Sometime in the night, gaffer. No one saw them arrive if you can believe that?! Real strange this whole thing, I'm tellin' you. Whoever heard of an orca round here?*

That afternoon, Old Dave ventured up to the cliff edges again to take another look, stopping every few minutes to catch his breath. The whole grassy area at the top was covered with people who had been joined by mobile coffee wagons and food stalls and TV and radio crews. Sealed-off areas of tents and semi-permanent structures had been hastily erected in the wind. *Too much*, exclaimed Old Dave as he decided to turn around and head back home. Another helicopter passed him on the way down to his hut, a makeshift hammock swinging underneath with a dead orca for cargo.

Tales from the Tide

That night, Dave wandered along the coastal path to the Spyglass but turned away when he saw the crowds outside. His joints ached too much to stand, and besides, all this to-do had left him feeling flat and exhausted; the cold of the storm had cut right through to the marrow of his old bones.

The next morning, the old man didn't wake 'til it was almost lunchtime. Not even the sound of the helicopters roused him. Angus whined and pawed at the latch beside the salt-smudged window on the front door. *Alright, lad,* he mumbled, coughing uncontrollably when he finally awoke, *alright. We'll be out soon.* By the time he was on the path again, hunched over, wheezing, and cold, it was early afternoon.

The cordon had been moved further back and this time there were three policemen manning it. *No access, sir,* one said with a hand raised. *This area is closed to the public. How did you get down here?* Old Dave leant on his walking stick, pausing for breath. *I live on the coastal path, squire. Not been up the cliff face today. Just wanted to check on how those orcas are doing - bloody shame this whole thing.* The policeman exhaled loudly. *The orcas?* he replied. *They got airlifted out yesterday - all dead. They're old news. We had four humpback whales arrive sometime early this morning. All lined up neatly in a row - a whole different problem.*

Old Dave gingerly picked his way back up the path until he reached the top. Makeshift seating had been set up, and he gratefully collapsed onto a bench. The cliff top was a hive of activity and the air above him thronging with helicopters and drones, but the sight below was incredible. Each of the whales' sleek, dark-grey backs flashed in the sunlight and was adorned with a mosaic of patches and patterns, as if they were living works of art. Their bodies, colossal yet carved with such care, funnelled down before fanning out into giant flukes. These once strong, graceful appendages now flat and lifeless like everything else on that beach. *It just ain't right*, Old Dave muttered, shaking his head, and pulling out a handkerchief.

The old man had fallen asleep after returning home and, when he awoke, was shivering with limbs that felt like lead. He looked at his watch, then over at the phone by the stove, and spent the next hour summoning his last reserves of energy in order to venture back out into the storm. The Spyglass was bustling when he arrived, the insides alive with talk of the whales and the week and what might come next, but the old man managed to secrete himself into a space at the bar. After ordering his pint, he warmed his stiff, mottled fingers so they could operate the tiny buttons, painstakingly pressed call and, pushing the thing close to his ear, heard 'you have one new message'.

beep Hello, Dad. Just thought I'd check in and see how you're getting on? I heard about those whales on the news and I thought of you. I can't believe it's happening at Steephill! I know I haven't called for a while; it's been really busy here and these last few months have flown by. Anyway, hope it's not causing too much fuss for you, and perhaps once it's all over we can talk about trying to meet up. Look, I've got to go but I'll try and call again soon. I know you can only get signal at the pub - when will they join the twenty-first century down there? Alright, speak soon, bye. *beep*

Through the pain in his knuckles, Old Dave methodically switched off the phone and returned it to his pocket. As he finished his pint, he silently smiled and nodded to himself, wiping a tear from his cheek before tilting back the bar stool and beginning the arduous journey home.

The next morning, when the emergency rescue teams and camera crews and visitors all clamoured to see what had washed up that day at Steephill Cove, they were disappointed to find that the answer was - nothing. Nothing except a single piece of weather-beaten old driftwood that nobody noticed. An

The Coastal Path

anonymous piece of a distant ship long sailed, pulled apart from its source and drawn and battered by the ocean waves until it was entirely unremarkable and almost unidentifiable.

On the coastal path, Angus had pawed at the latch all morning and eventually managed to get out on his own. When one of the workers on the beach recognised him and took him back, the front door was still open. After knocking a few times, he entered the hut to find an old man in bed, lifeless, cold and alone, with his head tilted to the side and his eyes wide open.

Feedback

A Wyndhamesque science fiction tale highlighting an ecological issue. It features a clear, straightforward writing style which strengthens its fantastical subject matter. The interwoven narrative of the man growing progressively weaker and his longing to hear from his son gives the story poignancy, and offers a personal note to a tale with a potentially global impact. Like all good science fiction stories, it leaves the reader with more questions than answers. What was the 'lacquer'? Did the man die of old age or because he'd walked on the beach?

Tales from the Tide

The Man, the Boy and the Sea
by Charlie Robinson

The road to San Nicholas had a capacity for treachery and the mountains appeared complicit. It wound its way down a steep slope to the sea and there it ended.

They had gambled on the mercy of mother nature several times but this was the storm season and she had taunted them. On the road and the sea, she had forbidden them entrance to both recently. *He* guided the van around the final hairpin and as the bay came into view, they saw the weight of the ocean heave itself against the land. The death throes of some huge storm, far out in the Atlantic, determined that their style of fishing was nigh impossible.

The Spanish called them 'Pesca Submarina' – underwater fishermen.

The older one's face was set in sombre thought. This was their fourth frustrating visit. The creased lines along his forehead suggested his mood and so, the boy kept quiet.

He brought the van to halt above the harbour. It was time to walk and survey the sea. This was their ritual.

The Man, the Boy and the Sea

They walked to the water's edge passing an old man. His weather-beaten face grinned out at them from beneath a battered, straw hat, 'Bravo, he said, 'rough' was his meaning, they nodded back at him.

On the harbour wall a crane stood, isolated and defiant as the dark foaming mass of water crashed over it. There was a headland to the north that made up that side of the bay, it was there the ocean rose and fell against the cliffs by thirty or forty feet. Fear is a strange companion.

'I'm going in,' *he* said and looked at his young friend. 'I don't expect you to.'

There is a point where fear can paralyse you, unless you control it. They had reached that point many times before, but the younger one was still learning and needed to know real fear.

'I'll go.'

'You don't have to.'

'I'll go.'

With the decision made they moved quickly. Donning the wetsuits that were made for the sport, black always black, sinking like shadows through the gloom.

When they were ready, they walked back to the harbour wall, passing the old man again.

'Loco.' He said shaking his head.

Another, much younger man, had joined him with a fresh but equally weathered face.

'Hey, amigos,' he shouted. 'Ingles?'

'That's right,' they called through the wind.

'Es no possible, the sea, she will not forgive a mistake today, eh?'

They raised their arms in the typical Latin gesture that says, 'what will be will be.'

'Good luck, amigos,' he said.

'Loco,' the old man repeated.

It was now that the instructions were given.

'Wait for the big wave,' *he* said.

They worked on the principle that every seventh wave was a big one. Some people disputed that, but it worked for them and so, they trusted it.

'Wait for it to roll back and then we go. Get in the water before it drops beyond the harbour wall. Swim and don't look around, just get away from the wall. Stay with me, go where I go and dive just off from me. It will be murky. Visibility will be down to six feet.' *He* was talking quickly now, his voice raised above the noise of the ocean. 'With all this activity the fish will be feeding. If there are any holes try looking in them.'

The younger one's mouth was too dry to speak, so he nodded frantically.

He continued. 'I'm aiming for the headland, watch the current it will carry you away from the shore and out to sea,' *he* grinned. 'Ready?' *he* asked.

There was a gallows grin from the younger one. They spat in their masks and washed them in a pool that had formed nearby, to prevent condensation. It took a long time to find the spit.

'Remember stay with me!' and *he* ran. The big wave hit the harbour wall, crashed over the crane, and began to recede. They jumped as far out as they could, every inch counted. They dropped fifteen, maybe twenty feet and swam hard. The fear gone. Survival had taken over.

They made good time to the headland.

'Dive the holes,' *he* said and was gone.

Deep under the turbulent water, in the cliff face there were holes. Fish like the mighty Grouper and smaller, but the equally palatable, Red Mullet would rest in them.

After three dives the younger one found himself alone. He looked for *him* but the swell was too great. He was either in a trough or on the crest of a wave and he could only see on a crest.

On his fourth descent he saw a gap in the rock. It was large enough to slide into, spear gun first, he entered. His eyes adjusted to the gloom, and he saw him. Grouper, big, black, and deep as a Grouper can be. He thought about how long he had been under. On a good easy dive, he had a two-minute bottom time at seventy-five feet, but this wasn't a good easy dive and he guessed he had less than a minute left. His spear was pointing at the Grouper's belly. He needed a head shot for a fish in a hole or it would go deeper, out of his reach to painful meaningless death. He moved and fired at the same time, the spear passing through the fish's head, killing him instantly. He pulled on the line but it was tight and he swore, as he realised the spear was lodged in the rocks. Swallowing repeatedly, his lungs searched in vain for oxygen. There was no choice he released the gun and began to push himself out of the hole.

But something pushed him back in. A huge force rammed him from behind and he was pinioned against the roof of the hole. He pushed back to no avail. Starting to feel light headed he knew if he didn't get air soon, he would black out. Suddenly the force ceased as quickly as it had begun and he was free of it. He scrambled out and finned to the surface with his lungs aching.

His head broke the surface, he blew hard, clearing the seawater from the snorkel and let the air flood in. Fear had taken him. His eyes were stinging from the tears. The pounding of his heart, in harmony with the raging ocean, left him weak. He needed to get out but there was nowhere to go. What was it that had just tried to drown him? He looked towards the mainland and saw it. A huge wave, the biggest he had ever seen, crashed into the harbour. He had to take control. His friends voice echoed in his head.

'Panic and you die. Control your fear or it will kill you,' he had said.

Taking bearings from the mainland he fought to get his breathing under control whilst maintaining his position. Then he went back down, fighting with the current, he heaved himself down through the gloom five times before he found the hole again. The spear was still lodged, and he was exhausted. He had been in the water for four hours and reluctantly decided to cut his losses. On the next dive into the hole, he cut the line, slid the Grouper from the spear and returned to the surface with both gun and fish intact.

The swim back was complicated by the way the current ran. He was a mile from the landing point and constantly lost his bearings due to the current dragging him away from the shore. It was a long arduous swim, and he began to wonder where his mentor would be. He hadn't seen him for three hours. Sometime later he felt something grab his shoulder, He turned and saw *him* at his side.

'Stay with me this time it will be harder getting out than it was getting in,' *he* said.

Tales from the Tide

They swam hard for an hour, constantly correcting their course. Eventually they were just off the harbour and *he* turned.

'I go first and you come when I wave you in and come in fast.'

He went in on a big wave and it lifted *him* onto the harbour wall, just as quickly the sea retreated leaving a twenty-five-foot drop before the next wave crashed in. The younger one waited whilst *he* counted him in. On *his* signal, he swam at the harbour wall feeling the mass of water welling up behind him. He glanced up and saw *him* signalling him back, either too slow or the wave hadn't been big enough. Turning he began to fin back out to sea. They started again and this time they got it right, the big wave dropped him onto the harbour as gently as a mother laying her baby in cot. They began to sort themselves out. A crowd had gathered around them, there were small children with that curious look on their faces. The men were examining the fish. The Grouper and Red Mullet of *his*. There was a good atmosphere and the old man with the straw hat beckoned to them.

'This man is the patron of the bar and he wishes to buy your fish,' the old man said, motioning to a short fellow with a round smiling face. 'You are tired so we will carry your fish to the bar. When you are rested

The Man, the Boy and the Sea

join us in the bar, he will pay you, and he will give you a good price.'

They agreed, and the crowd headed up the hill towards the van, there were many questions.

'Where did you find the fish?'

'How deep did you go?'

The children asked if they had been scared. Children, always curious about fear. They answered that, of course they had been scared and the old man said it was good for a man to be scared sometimes.

'To know fear is to know the sea,' he said.

His leathery face was close and his bright blue eyes were penetrating, searching. The younger one shivered and the old man nodded and walked away. When they reached the van the crowd left them and continued up the hill to the bar.

They made coffee.

'You won,' *he* said.

'You mean I beat the sea?'

'No, you defeated yourself. The sea is inanimate, it doesn't think or feel but you do. You defeated your inner-self. The part of us that wants to quit and go running home to our mothers. Life is an experience. Today was just another notch on your life pole.' *He* grinned.

After the coffee they went to the bar.

Tales from the Tide

The patron came out from behind his counter to greet them. He told them the fish were beautiful and had dressed out well. He complimented their marksmanship and paid them a fair price. They took two stools at the bar and ordered beer. A woman appeared from the kitchen carrying a huge plate of fish.

'My wife has dressed them, please, choose one each,' said the patron.

A little bemused they both selected the Red Mullet. She returned later with the cooked fish accompanied by potatoes boiled with garlic in a way that only the Spanish do well. The patron smiled.

'Eat, enjoy,' he said.

They finished their meal and there was much talk of bravado, rough seas and of course the fishing. As they were leaving the old man took the younger one to a side, he looked grave.

'Today you have learnt not to fear the sea. You must never fear the sea,' he said. 'Nor must you underestimate her. But you must respect her. You are young and today maybe you underestimated her, maybe you showed her disrespect and maybe you didn't, that is not for me to say. Whatever you did today she forgave you. Be careful young one. She does not forgive often and rarely does she forgive twice.' Then, grinning he walked away.

The Man, the Boy and the Sea

Feedback

A story with a definite Hemingway influence, including the title. It has a strong first paragraph that foreshadows what is to come, particularly with the use of the words: treachery, complicit, death throes. I felt I knew who the man, and the boy were partly because of the immediate Hemingway influence and partly because of the dialogue - or lack of it. They are doers not talkers. The telling of that action, of underwater fishing and the struggle in the cave put this story in the top ten. I particularly liked the technical detail of how the boy spat into his mask before putting it on to avoid condensation but had trouble making spit. The author told us the boy was scared without telling us the boy was scared. Although I do think it was a good decision not to name anyone, I did get confused over who was 'he', the older one, the old man, and the much younger man. But a little light editing should sort that out, perhaps replacing 'he' and 'him' with 'the man' throughout. Ultimately, this is a Hemingwayesque bullfighting story - but with a Grouper.

The Sea
by Fran Pridham

She shoved hard against the door to open it. It needed repairing. Something shaved off where the sea breezes had swollen the wood. But then everything needed repainting and replacing so what was the point? She was the only one who used the hut now anyway. Helen and Paul would sell it, when she was gone, and that would be that.

She swam every day, so the dull November morning wasn't a problem. The sun melted its sorbet yellow into the sky and although the promenade was grey and empty and the air fresh, it was dry. No one would think it odd that she'd gone for a swim, though they might question the early hour, or why she'd crept out and left Steve on his own. They'd probably think, 'How selfish!' even though she'd locked his bedroom door and left the carer a note.

She slumped onto the bench and shut her eyes, feeling the wood of the hut behind her back and breathing in the comfort of its familiar salt. The hut was so basic, she really should have kept it in a better condition. An ancient camping gas stove stood on the

The Sea

sideboard and she was half tempted to make herself a cup of tea but then couldn't find the energy, besides she hadn't brought any milk with her. She'd strip in a minute and get out there. Meanwhile, the bag with her towel and swimming things rested on her lap.

'Do you think this is working, Mum?' Her daughter's tense voice echoed in her head. 'I know you're doing your best, Mum, but he was in the street! No shoes on, wandering down the street.'

It had been a mistake to tell her. Of course, Helen would be angry.

She'd mumbled, 'I just nodded off.' And was cross with herself for sounding so weak, so defensive. She'd sat down to watch Countdown and woken up on the settee with a start, her head thumping and drool oozing its way onto the cushion. Steve hadn't gone far, but he'd still had enough time to find his way out onto the street.

'There's no point discussing this, is there? You know what I think.' She could imagine her daughter's frown, her stiff lips almost spitting the words out. 'This is not loving him,' and then she'd ended the call and switched the phone off.

Perhaps Helen was right.

She forced her eyes open, put the bag down and pulled her T shirt over her head. She should have saved herself some effort and put her swimming costume on when she got dressed. Her body sagged, her breasts like abandoned tea bags, dried, old. She sat there for a moment and felt a sigh shiver over her exposed skin. Instinctively she leant forward and switched on the Calor gas heater, positioned to spread its warmth over her on mornings like this.

She was so tired. She could hear the sea, its rhythmic slap and drag of shingle just beyond the hut, its grey cold waiting for her. Through the window she saw a seagull, perched on the breakwater. Its orange claws, broken and twisted with age, clasped the wood firmly; its head erect and firm, its beak pointed towards the sea, its beady eye drinking in the waves gently rising and dipping in the bay. A single bird, its shape clear against the light blue sky.

She stood up pulled her track suit trousers down, slipped off her pants and scrabbled in her bag for her costume. Why had she brought a towel? Such a creature of habit. But taking a towel swimming was normal, so it was a good thing. She pulled her costume on. Like her body it sagged and hung on her like loose skin. She should have bought a new one years ago though it didn't really matter. No one ever saw her costume as she swam across the bay.

She sat down again, the towel piled on her lap, the warm air from the fire giving out enough heat to tempt her into staying where she was. Perhaps she should

The Sea

have had some breakfast. Something to give her a boost but she'd just take her time. Just do this at her own pace.

Helen did have a point. Holding onto someone wasn't really about love. 'Life is a casting off.' So depressing, nothing but loss. She'd cried when her kids left home, cried when they'd come back and cried when they went away again. Always change and shifting and never being sure what she was supposed to be. Now Helen seemed to think she was the child.

And Paul wasn't very different. He phoned regularly, 'How are you? How's Dad?' Always sympathetic but sorry he couldn't help because of the distance to travel, his important job, his family. He probably didn't realise every call seemed to end with the mantra, 'Dad knows you love him. He wouldn't want it to be like this.'

So how was Paul so sure what Dad wanted? So sure too about what she should feel when she wasn't even sure herself what she felt about anything anymore? She couldn't bring herself to tell them she even wondered sometimes if she still loved Steve. Had she ever really loved him? He'd certainly driven her mad at times.

Take the hut. He'd known how much it meant to her, the only thing she'd inherited from her family and she used it every day but did he help her sort it out?

Give it a lick of paint even? Too late now. Her mouth stiffened into a hard line.

In the past she and her sisters had fought each other for space as they'd changed in the hut for swimming. And the parties they'd had there, carrying sandwiches and huge basins of red jelly and pink blancmange to share into plastic bowls that she'd kept, still stacked in the wooden cupboard in the corner. As a child she'd loved the sucking sound of jelly being spooned out of the large basin and the feel and taste of it as she'd rolled it round her mouth and to suck into a liquid before swallowing. Disgusting. Mum always just laughed, 'Enjoy! A party's not a party without jelly.'

For years now, the hut hadn't seen any parties and despite repeatedly trying to tempt him to join her there, Steve had rarely come. Did she love him? She must have done once. They'd been together for years. It must have been love. When he'd first started to slip she hadn't really understood. He'd always been so sure of himself, irritatingly so, and suddenly their arguments changed. Instead of hearing herself insisting, 'Let me do it my way,' she found herself encouraging him out of his insecurity, his passivity, coaxing him with, 'What do you think? How should we do it?'

And the triggers that signalled change after change. The day he'd handed the car keys to her mumbling, 'I

The Sea

think you'd better drive.' The day he'd tried to put his coat on back to front. The day he couldn't find the word for lift.

She sighed. None of that mattered. She could still feel the softness of his hand in hers and even now if at night she snuggled close to him in bed she felt safe. In the dark, moulded to his warm body, moving gently to the rhythm of his breathing she felt comforted. They were just together as they'd always been. She wasn't sure now how to be on her own.

Enough. She stood up and stretched her arms above her head, her bingo wings irritating her. She just couldn't be bothered with all this thinking. She was old herself. Why did people think she wanted to sort everything out and make all the plans? Why bother. With renewed determination she picked up her track suit bottoms and T shirt, folded them and piled them neatly on the bench, then turned off the fire.

The freshness of the air momentarily took her aback when she opened the door and looked out at the beach. The dusty pebbles tumbled against each other right up to the door and she slipped her battered leather sandals on before she stepped out. Her feet had grown increasingly sensitive with age and she no longer felt any desire to run across the stones and throw herself recklessly into the waves.

Tales from the Tide

Reaching the sea, she let the water run over her toes. Freezing. For a moment the cold made her pause. Then she waded in, pushing her thin body against the water's weight until she stood waist deep as the cold shocked its way through her. She knew how to do this. In one quick movement she pointed her arms into a triangle above her head and then plunged them into the water, letting it stream over her body as she pushed herself off the stony bottom, her head briefly dipping into the sea, her mouth gasping for air as she raised it again and gave herself a moment to let the brain freeze subside. Cold stunned every muscle as her arms pushed herself out towards the horizon. Soon feeling would return and tingle its way through her limbs but even before that moment the water flowing across her body flooded her with the relief felt at coming home. She dipped her head, turned it, took a breath and let her arms and legs move her body in a clear line out away from the pebbled shore and towards the yellow sun melting into the pale horizon. In the still calm of the early morning, her limbs felt suspended in the waves' lullaby.

She would deliberately ignore her mother's advice burnt into her as a child, 'Never swim beyond the scout boat.' It still bobbed gently in the water, anchored at the place where the bay opened out to the sea. But as feeling came back into her numb body in a series

The Sea

almost of electric shocks so too did the familiar awe and fear. She knew the sea was a dangerous friend even as muscle memory ploughed her body forward stroke after stroke.

As she tasted salt in her mouth, she suddenly realised it came partly from her tears. She let them fall, to trickle into the sea that moulded to her as she rose and fell in the gentle waves. The cold ebbed away from her body and soft rain drifted down to caress her face. She heard seagulls cawing above her and saw the birds twisting together on the wind in mysterious patterns as they circled in the sky.

She was sure of one thing. Her body ached with pleasure in the cold of the sea, her limbs taunt her breath rapid but reaching deep into her. She was in the sea and somehow the sea was within her. As the scout boat loomed close, loops of wet rope bumping against its battered hull, she reached up her hand to hold onto one. She paused for breath, soaking in the uncompromising slate blue sea which supported her, as she looked to the horizon where the water met the pale blue sky. A deep silence filled her.

Suddenly decisive, she turned towards the shore. Stroke by stroke, she pulled her body back, her arms steady, her legs strong, her mind still and certain. It wouldn't take her long to reach the beach hut, to dress

and return home and then wake Steve with his early morning coffee.
She'd take Steve with her to buy what she needed, and they could go on to the beach. Then she'd paint the hut bright yellow, the same colour Mum had painted it in the party days.

Feedback

There were several stories of wives with ill/abusive/dead husbands, including several in which women recall memories of better times. What set this story apart was the way in which those memories (and present day problems) were skilfully interwoven into the action of the woman changing into her swimming costume and the rich description of the things around her, including her own body. The woman is apparently contemplating suicide but the transformative power of the beach hut changes her mind, and the ending of the story is upbeat - as it should be - and places it in the top ten. In many ways, this story is a 'homecoming' tale but to a childhood home (via the hut and the sea) not the one she has just left, with her husband locked in the bedroom. There was more than one story entitled 'The Sea'. I suggest renaming this, perhaps as 'The Sea/Beach Hut'.

Anne Funnell Members' Shield

Members of the Norwich Writers' Circle can nominate one of their entries for consideration in the Anne Funnell Members' shield.

Anne was a long standing member of the Circle who passed away in 2022. A prolific author of romantic novels, she held the posts of Chair and President.

1st Place
Breaking Through
by Samantha Mattocks

I unzipped my tent and took a deep breath, waiting for the sea air to fill my lungs. My eyes moved up to the skies, looking for the gulls and petrels swooping overhead. To my surprise, neither happened. No mews, no salty tang. Silence.

I stood and stepped out onto the shoreline, anticipating the whispering crash as the waves hit the sand. Instead, a shard of something sharp bit into the sole of my boot. I registered a crackle. A glance out to sea revealed magic had happened overnight. Instead of tidal ebbs and flows, ice was gently shifting before me. The ink-black sea that I had seen last night in the fading light had frozen in the cold.

I took a tentative step onto the frozen waves, hearing another crackle of ice as my weight shifted. Another step, and the frost quake resounded around me. It was beautiful. It was eerie. I wanted to run and tell the world to come and look at this phenomenon before me. And yet, I was angry. Disappointed. For

Breaking Through

this was not what I wanted. This was not why I had travelled on trains and traipsed along undulating roads to reach this point.

I came to the sea for answers, and overnight, those answers vanished, frozen away. Instead of the writhing waters of froth and foam that would throw what I needed at my feet for me to pick through as I chose, I had a void of sea ice before me, blanketing the secrets below.

With a sigh, I looked to the skies vast above me. I realised all I could hear was the gentle crunch of the moving sea of ice. There were no birds, no animal cries from the pine forest nearby. Just silence.

Maybe this was my answer.

I took another step out onto the ice, something else registering above my disappointment. Cold. Surprisingly, it didn't feel freezing, although clearly it was. Exhaling, I enjoyed the sight of smokeless vapours coming from my mouth. I relished in the shock of frosty air drawing deep into my lungs. I felt lifted by the energy this depth of cold gave. Despite my desire for anger at the injustice of nature, I couldn't help but feel calm.

Another step. And another. The musical crackle of ice created its own song, calling to the sirens to come and take me away. Help me keep on running despite my source of solace being frozen.

Tales from the Tide

Frozen. Just as I had been. Putting up the perfect boundary against the blows that rained down upon me. Verbal, mostly. The snide remark. A vicious snap of words against my ears, said in anger and hate. The quelling look that silenced me in a room full of friends. Friends who could not see what was happening. Did not want to see. Would look no further than the ice clinking in their glasses. I wonder what they would make of this – enough ice for their drinks to blindside them to everything.

It was the punch that broke my frozen state. His raised voice, the glassy look in his eyes from too much grain. The swiftly followed punch to the stomach. As I took another step out onto the impossible, walking on water, I felt comforted by the crunch of ice beneath me. I felt glad he had punched me, waking me from the depths of my ignorance. Pushing me to run.

Turning around, I saw I was already some distance from the shore, my open tent door flapping a pathetic hello in the gentle breeze. All around me, the sun danced on sea crystals, making the ice seem alive. It glittered and sparkled, virgin fresh waves of undulating ice tides. My heart lifted.

I closed my eyes, and my senses heightened. The cold around me became sharper as the wind picked up, and I could hear the sweeping rustle of pine trees beginning to bend and give in the strengthening breeze.

One step. That was all it took to change my world, one step towards the door and towards my unstoppable future.

Don't look back.

The wind whipped up again, and I could sense the skies darkening over. As I glanced at the whispering pines, I took another step. There was a hard crack. It sounded like a muffled bullet leaving the barrel of a gun. I felt panic overwhelm me, as the sea beneath me started its fight against the ice blanket above.

For despite the appearance of calm, the sea below never stopped moving. The water still flowed, and the tides continued to follow their celestial guides. The bullet-like crack had torn a line through the ice barrier, revealing the grey navy waters below.

I shivered.

Panic set in as I made for shore, each step a risk. All that was between me and the cold waters was a layer of ice that was dissolving.

Focus.

I looked at my tent, fluttering against the zephyr. It was my safe place, my guide, my focus.

Step by step. Making each footfall as light as I could, desperate to avoid falling into the cold waters and being dragged under the icy waves that would prevent me from getting out. Just as my denial had prevented me from escaping before.

One more step. Just one more. And then one more again.

My foot stepped down. And down. And down.

I plunged, left side first, through the melting ice and into the freezing arms of the sea below. My mouth, open in a cry, quickly filled with the ink-black liquid as, before I knew it, I was under. Under the ice. Enveloped by water.

My fists smacked against the ice, causing ripples of bubbles and tiny cracks. Cracks only a nudibranch could get through if they could survive in this darkening light.

My lungs felt ready to burst as I continued to hold my breath, fruitlessly battering against the glass above. It seemed my weight was heavier on earth than in the sea, and I felt powerless as I banged and smashed above me as I fell below.

Now sodden, my clothes dragged me down and I wriggled out of my jacket, kicked off my boots, hastily thrown on this morning. As they headed for their watery bed, I rose once more and pushed against the semi-frozen waves with all my might. Just as I gave up hope, a hole appeared. Not huge, but big enough.

I put one hand up and grabbed hold of the side, pulling myself towards the air above.

Breaking Through

With a shuddering, coughing breath, I gasped. Air painfully filled my lungs as water ran from my mouth.

Frozen to the spot, I dare not move an inch and risk taking away my connection to the world above.

Deep breaths.

Breathe deeply.

Calm.

I realised I was moving, the tidal surges trying to take me further from the shore. I could feel the water swirling around my legs, feet brushing against things unknown below. Normally this would be my worst nightmare, things I cannot see, but somehow, I had ended up in a living dream of a different kind. A vital dream, resulting in life – or death.

Helpless against the currents, I thought back, back to that moment I registered something more than ire in his eyes. As his fist hit my body, pushing me off balance and onto the cold tiled floor, my flight or fight system kicked in. Now, one day later, I needed to summon that feeling again.

With urgency, I flayed my hands around the icy window to my escape route. I didn't care that it hurt and stung; if anything, each dent and slice to my hands reaffirmed my desire to live.

I realised that, with each punch, I was screaming. A visceral scream that came from the very core of my being. My feet were kicking, treading the water as the ice receded and I could finally crawl out of the inky grave I had almost found myself in.

I lay on the ice, stretched out and panting, staring at the skies above. One lone petrel came into view, soaring on the thermals. I watched its pattern through the air as my breathing returned to normal and my heart stopped racing. Glancing down, I saw the ice had turned to rust as my battered hands, numb to the elements, bled on the pure white glaze.

Again, the ice cracked, a sharp sound that went straight through my head. I decided not to stand, and instead I rolled myself, one large level weight spread across the ice so as not to add pressure. I felt like a seal, rolling my frozen, soaked body over and over towards the shore.

Finally, the ice gave way to water, and I stood, waves lapping against my legs. I trudged through the last stretch and fell onto the sand. I stripped my clothes, pulled on dry jumpers and jeans, and curled up in my sleeping bag.

Sleep came quickly, overwhelming me as the last vestiges of ice ran from my hair.

The light woke me, the orange sun bouncing off the sea straight into my tent. I disentangled myself from my sleeping bag and staggered outside.

All the ice was gone. The waves were gently rolling across the sand. The gulls mewed overhead, looking for the last of the fish before they returned to their nests for the night.

As the sun sank towards the horizon, the sea changed colour from grey-tumbled aqua to blue to that dark navy that had enveloped me earlier. The reassuring sound of the waves calmed my mind, and I knew that the answers I needed were clearly there for me to see.

All was calm once more.

Feedback

It's not always easy to write a story with only one character, but this pulls it off. It's poetic and well written with some really nice description – I particularly liked "my tent door flapping a pathetic hello". It's atmospheric and the reader can feel the silence and the cold and wet, contrasting with the violent flashbacks.

2nd Place
The Once Golden Sea
by Iain Andrews

She'd only imagined what the ocean would be like. The young woman sat by the shore, entranced by the endless waves dancing from the horizon, bewitched by the symphony of the sea—the tenor of surf breaking on a pebbled beach, the soprano calls of a chorale of gulls.

She cried with palpable joy. 'It is beautiful.'

The old man sitting beside her on the bench grunted. This bleak stretch of Scotland's north-east coast was all he knew—a lifetime of fishing, poverty, friends lost to shipwreck, huts shattered by savage storms. Arthritis crippled his rough hands. Not that they needed to haul a net again. The outsiders had delivered the final blow, imposing crippling quotas on the fleet.

'You are lucky to live here,' she said.

'Ye think so?' He observed her for the first time. Her dark skin and hair suggested she'd travelled far.

The Once Golden Sea

The face suggested a woman in her twenties. Her eyes told him she'd suffered the cares of a lifetime. 'Why?'

'It is peaceful,' she replied.

'It's not always like this. Ye wouldna like it in the winter.'

She continued to stare at the sea. 'Is it dangerous?'

'Not if ye bide indoors.'

'Then I would still like it. I would stand by my window and watch.'

'There's too many men lost their lives out there.'

She turned and noticed the acquiescent sadness in his weather-worn face. The young woman had seen that look a thousand times in her homeland and refugee camps. War destroys as many dreams as lives.

'They were free to go, were they not?' she said.

'They'd not much choice.'

The woman peered at the sparkling waves again. 'They had a choice. Better than many.'

The old man glared at the stones smothered by rotting brown vegetation, surrounded by the detritus of civilisation: empty plastic bottles, tins, and cigarette packets. The stench of decaying seaweed, the unwanted spawn of storms, hung around him. He was just another discard rejected by the sea.

She saw the water playing among the rocks, the white birds soaring and swooping in the breeze, sculptured driftwood free to float to the furthest corners of the world.

'Where are ye from?' he asked.

'Iraq. A city called Mosul. You have heard of it?'

The name was familiar to him. He'd perhaps heard it on the news—or one of the locals served there in a war. 'Maybe. Why did ye leave?'

'My family was killed and my home destroyed. A cousin helped me to come to England.'

The old man kept staring at the cold sea. Did she know what country she'd come to?

His silence made her uncomfortable. 'Are you from here?'

'Aye, born and bred. A fisherman like my father and his father.'

'You must like it, to stay so long.'

He shook his head. 'Where else would I go? What else could I do?'

The woman found no answer. She would have gone anywhere, done anything, to escape the horrors of war and warped religion. But she didn't know this land. Perhaps there were invisible barriers, forces beyond her comprehension, keeping the old man tied to this town on the edge of the ocean.

His eyes hadn't left the leaden sea. A memory... another girl, another time... also pretty, different from this dark-skinned woman who sat where she once did.

The Once Golden Sea

Red-haired, freckled, a laugh like music. He married her and lived with her for fifty years before cancer stole her away. When the weather was cruel, she'd sit here with the other wives, staring at an ugly, angry swell, praying to an uncaring god that their men would return, cursing her lot as a fisherman's wife.

His mind drifted back to when they first walked out, hand in hand. They always came down to this shore, away from the streets of the town, grey with post-war austerity. He'd forgotten how he felt then, before the tides of age and misfortune washed away his happiness. The sun always shone in those memories, turning the crests of the waves golden at the end of each glorious summer day.

Now in late autumn, the sea lay under a shroud of cloud. Some predicted snow was due in the next week. Had the lass by his side ever seen snow? He'd never minded snow. It was the days when it was too cold for snow he'd hated. Those days when ice crusted treacherous decks, when all the weatherproof clothing in the world couldn't keep the chill from his bones.

The old man tore his gaze from the past and glanced at his companion. 'Where are ye staying?'

'I live with a family. The husband is from my country. He works in the oil industry.'

The old man grunted again. A few had benefited from oil, most had not. Some young men had smelt money and left the fishing to man supply vessels or train as roustabouts. Those that stayed saw their boats laid up and the price of houses rise beyond their means. The loveless union of prosperity and despair gave birth to streets scarred by decay, homelessness and drug addiction.

Outsiders weren't affected.

The Iraqi husband must be an outsider. The old man didn't despise him because he was foreign. Most of the outsiders who lived in the town were Scottish. They'd bought all the best houses, swallowing the estate agents' pitch that the town was 'quaint', 'picturesque' and 'full of character'. They spent their money in Aberdeen rather than in the few local shops that weren't charity outlets or bookmakers.

The girl was an outsider too.

'That's nice of them,' he said. 'Giving ye a home and all that.'

'I work as their nanny,' she said. Her smile faded. 'They found out I was... good with children.'

She brushed aside a tear and looked away. She wasn't the usual outsider, smug and patronising. Now it was her turn to scowl at the sea. She'd been happy when she arrived. He feared he'd infected her with his bitterness.

'I'm sorry,' he said. 'I shouldna ask so many questions.'

The Once Golden Sea

The woman forced a smile. 'No, it is not your fault. I am glad you have welcomed me to your country.'

He decided he wouldn't interrogate her any more, even though he was intrigued.

She answered his unspoken curiosity. 'I had my own children. A boy and a girl. I left them with my husband.' She stopped and wiped her eyes again. 'I had to buy bread. A rocket hit our house.'

The old man had a daughter. She lived in Glasgow and never called him. He'd never really bothered to get in touch with her after their final argument. Her last letter mentioned two grandsons. They'd be in their early teens by now. He had a connection to other human beings in this world. This girl couldn't even claim the comfort of that thought..

'I'm sorry.' He dared touch her on the arm.

'Don't be. You are not to blame. Your land has given me new life.'

'Will ye stay in the town?' he asked.

'I don't know. If your government grants me asylum, I will go to college. I would like to be a nurse.' A smile ghosted across her face again. 'Or perhaps I will be a midwife. I would help bring new beginnings, new happiness to the world. Who knows what I could do?'

She wore a sheepskin coat, probably borrowed. It was too big for her. Her hands were lost in matching mittens. Her dark hair hung long below a woollen hat. He wondered if Scotland might prove too cold for her. He dared not talk, in case he opened other wounds. They listened to the sounds of the sea.

'Why do you come here,' she asked at last, 'if you dislike the water?'

'I...' He hesitated. He didn't know. Did he come here to remember, or forget? Did he squat in this shelter, hoping he might have company, or even praying he would be left alone? His cramped cottage was no longer a home, but an empty shell where he slept and waited for death. There might be ghosts within his walls, but they offered no comfort. There were ghosts here too, but sometimes the living intruded. He often resented them as well. Either they reminded him of the past or represented a world that excluded him.

'I dinna ken,' he said at last.

'Perhaps your heart knows?'

New visions came into his head. He was laughing, a teenager with pals, pockets full of money, belly full of drink, dreams only of the future. He strolled again with his Jean, love and desire raging in his breast. He was running, chasing his three-year-old daughter, taking pleasure in her giggles and screams of delight.

He'd lost something along the way, and he realised the reason he kept returning to this spot was to find it.

The Once Golden Sea

She looked around with renewed wonder. 'I will never forget this place. It is magical.'

She gasped and pointed her arm towards the sea.

A dolphin leapt above the waves. Then a second. As he looked, perhaps five or six rose from the waters as the sun escaped from the clouds, transforming greyness into a kaleidoscope of blue and gold.

The old man blinked as if transported to an unexplored country. The sad, familiar ghosts of the past transmuted into spirits of hope.

He smiled at her. Perhaps the first time he'd smiled in years. She smiled back.

'Aye,' he said. 'Magical.'

He watched her leave. As she reached the path that led to the town, she turned and waved, almost as if she was beckoning him to walk away from this grey graveyard of lost hopes.

The old man turned back to the sea. The sun had once again retreated behind a wall of cloud while the dolphins had vanished. As he watched, the wind died and with it the waves, so he now gazed at a featureless wall of grey with no visible horizon.

Nothing lay out there. It was cold and empty, like his soul before the woman touched it with her joy, like the future he faced unless he overcame his demons. In a short time, the long darkness of night would envelop his world. The old man cast a last look at the once golden sea before turning his back on the ocean. He glanced at his watch. Time was no longer on his side. Hope had become his new companion.

He had to reach the coach station and find out the times of buses to Glasgow.

Feedback

A story of change and contrast, with a lovely interaction between two very different characters, from which they both gain something. There are some lovely descriptions of both the characters and their surroundings, and the very different ways people interpret the same thing. The title nicely reflects the story, and it has a great, hopeful ending.

3rd Place
The Eye of the Storm
by Simon Conner

The sailor clings weakly to the wreckage, clings to the fraying threads of consciousness. He lays on the few timbers, all that remain of the 'Lady Patricia'. The sun beats down and the salty-sea washes over him. The wreckage turns as it drifts, coursing in one current, then another. For days it carries him across the broad sea, in sight finally of land. An eastern shore of England, but upon which he will never walk. The sailor's eyes open wide, his cracked lips move, he whispers a parched entreaty, reaches out. But there is none to hear him, neither man nor God. As he exhales his last breath, a telescope slips from beneath his tattered shirt.

The telescope sinks, the brass gleaming as it turns, the dark optic glimmering, an implacable eye.

*

Joseph and Ted set sail on the morning tide before dawn, as they do every morning, except for Sundays of course. After stabling Snowy, Rose walks to the denes up at Yarmouth's north beach, to watch the sun rise over the sea and enjoy the solitude in the wide expanse of sand and dune. A chill wind is blowing off the North Sea, ruffling her skirts. Rose pulls her shawl closer but it is a glorious spring morning, the new light luminous over the water. She watches white clouds drift from the horizon, like great sailing ships coming to port. Passing momentarily across the sun, they leave pools of light so that the yellow of the shoals becomes visible beneath the broiling waves – sandbanks to snare the unwary. She had grown up on tales of wrecks within sight of the beach, most famously *The Gloucester*, carrying a future King. Almost two hundred years ago but still marked in memory.

"Aye a perilous stretch of sea," the fishermen nod sagely.

The sand shines where the waters recede at the shore's edge. Rose laughs at the little Dunlins scurrying back and forth from the pushing-pulling waves that susurrate over a stretch of stranded shingle. And then she sees it, half hidden in the wet sand, glistening in the light. Rose picks up the telescope. She looks around, certain that the owner must be looking to reclaim this valuable piece, but she is alone. Rose brushes off the sand. The telescope is heavy, solid, gleaming – "beautiful," she whispers, "father will be right pleased, it'll help find the catch." A distant rumble booms across the deep. Rose looks to the horizon where a dark line foreshadows a coming change. She holds the telescope tight within her shawl and walks quickly towards the south beach to meet her father and brother returned from the morning's fishing, excited to deliver up her prize.

*

The untethered sail flaps in the gentle spring breeze. The briny air is mixed with the smell of oily fish and tar creating a pungent aura around *The Bethany*. The boat rests heavily on the beach where Snowy has hauled it out of the surf. "Father look, see what I found up at the denes this morning," Rose proudly holds out the shiny instrument. Joseph looks up from the creel he is filling. "It'll help spy out the silver darlin's before ever you put to sea," she says. "You'll see the oil shine on the surface father, and the gulls all clamoured about."

"I never needed no glass to find the herring afore Rose," he replies, not taking the telescope from her. "And where did it come from, eh? A wreck I don't wonder. Another man's curse will come on us mark you. Them waters is dangerous enough without poking at ill fortune."

"But father…"

"I'll not take it gal. Not to sea, you hear me."

Rose looks pleadingly at her father but his face is closed as he continues loading the creels.

"Such nonsense!" she thinks, but knows that her father, like all fishermen, are quick to their superstitions. Rose sits miserably in the prow of *The Bethany*, looking through the telescope to the horizon. She watches the great navy ships dressed in full sail, heading to faraway places that she can only imagine. But her heart isn't in it. Ted is on the beach by the prow mardlin' away but Rose is not listening.

I'll not take it gal. Not to sea, you hear me.
*

Nothing more is said about the telescope the next day as Joseph and Ted launch on the morning tide. Rose walks gloomily back to the north denes. She had been so excited finding the telescope and then so unhappy that her father could not, *would* not see the advantage. Rose's father is in thrall to the implacable might of the sea, its fast moods. She knows this, accepts that these stubborn men are slow to change, fearful even. But sometimes, like now, it drives her mad. She can hear their cautious refrain:

"*We'll do what we have always done, in the ways it has always been done, us, our fathers afore us, our grandfathers...*"

"Ha!" she stamps her foot in frustration. There is a sudden change in the light. Rose notices that the

The Eye of the Storm

horizon is darkening. A storm is gathering, a big one. She can feel the drama waiting to unfold, the sea and sky ready to do battle. Rose remembers lines from *The Rime of the Ancient Mariner* they read at school. She shouts across the squalling sea –

And now the storm-blast came, and he
Was tyrannous and strong:
He struck with his o'ertaking wings,
And chased us south along.

As if in answer there is deep rumble from across the water. Rose watches great storm clouds billowing out over the North Sea. They rise like dark bruises from the horizon and vault to the heavens in biblical grandeur. The sky is black over the water but the sun still shines from the west through pale, pillowy clouds, reaching from over the land. The shimmering surface of the wet sand reflects back the darkening sky and mirrors the white of a sail, that of a fishing boat urging back to shore before the storm breaks. Rose notices that many other boats are already drawn up on the beach. They stand like sentinels, waiting, watching, as the light and dark prepare their struggle for dominion.

"Father," she frowns, "and Ted. Have they come to shore?" Rose must hurry down to the south beach. As she turns, a great roll of thunder booms across the dark and troubled sea. The storm's fury is finally unleashed.

*

Tales from the Tide

"Not seen as great a storm as that for forty year or more," the retired and toothless fishermen intone as they gather at the jetty, like a flock of raggedy gulls scavenging on scraps of news. The implacable sea has ravaged the shoreline, taking boats that weren't far enough beyond its greedy reach. Huts have been smashed to sticks and families living under upturned boats are now homeless. There is no sign of her father – *The Bethany* is not in its usual place down from the jetty, nor anywhere else on the beach.

Mr. Lacon, the lifeboat skipper, is in deep conversation with the crew. They are trying to account for everyone amidst all the confusion, any that might not have made it to shore before the storm.

"Hello young Rose, what's amiss," Mr. Lacon can see her distress.

"Mr Lacon, it's father and Ted, they should've been back on the tide some two hours ago," she falters, "but the storm…"

"Aye Rose, well your father, Joseph, he's an experienced fisherman," Peter Lacon says gently, concealing his own concern. "He'll likely be back in the twilight with a right big catch," He smiles reassuringly.

Rose looks at him pleadingly. "Can't you…"

"As you rightly know Miss Rose," Mr Lacon interrupts, "we cannot go out in the dark, that wouldn't

The Eye of the Storm

help anyone now would it gal?" Rose nods, the tears in her eyes reflect the last of the day. "Look you Rose, I'm sure they'll be back, but if not, then me and the crew, we'll be here afore first light, all ready to set out."

*

Rose keeps a lonely vigil that night, straining into the darkness. Time after time she imagines she sees something, hears the flap of a sail, the slap of water on the hull of a boat. But it is a wave, or a gull, or a seal. In the first rumour of light, as the horizon begins to separate the sea and sky, Rose puts the telescope to her eye. Nothing. Horizon to horizon. Nothing.

*

Rose watches from the shore as the lifeboat launches into the surf, Mr Lacon waves in her direction. The sun is rising into a blue sky. The sea is calm now, exhausted after the effort of the great storm. Other boats, those still whole, are setting out, giving truth to the adage: 'time and tide wait for no man' – there are fish to be caught and sold at market, food to be put on the table. Life goes on. Rose feels the strangeness of a normal day; the tranquillity of a bright, calm sea, belying the dark, turbulent depths of her anguish.

Nine hours searching. The lifeboat returns to shore in the failing light. There was some wreckage out near

Scroby Sands but not enough to know if it was *The Bethany*. They found no one in the water, alive or…

"I'm right sorry gal." Peter Lacon can offer Rose no comfort.

Neighbours are kindly but their words fall deaf upon Rose's ears. She trudges across the infinity of the beach, back to the empty house in the narrow Rows. It is cold there, and dark. Quiet. A stillness as deep as the ocean. Rose finds the telescope is still in her grasp. "Father was right. I did this. Brought down the curse upon us." She turns, leaves the house and walks resolutely across the beach back to the shoreline. Rose lifts the telescope above her head and screams as she throws it as hard and as far as she can. She falls to her knees weeping, clutching at the wet sand. The cold sea laps at her skirts, all hope ebbing with the receding tide.

The telescope sinks, the brass gleaming as it turns, the dark optic glimmering, an implacable eye.

*

Jenny loves walking alone on the North Denes, keeping well away from the 'kiss-me-quick' crowds. They flock to Yarmouth every summer and are so-o-o uncool. So thinks Jenny and all her mates. The tourists endlessly feed the slot machines, gorge on fish-and-chips and candy-floss. They watch faded comedians on the pier and head for the second, no, *third* rate rides

The Eye of the Storm

at the lame Pleasure Beach, at the south-end beyond Peggotty Road. But today, black clouds and the threat of a storm ensure Jenny's solitude in the expansive Denes. She flip-flops along the beach in her favourite polka dot swimsuit, a towel around her waist, "for modesty young lady," her mother had insisted. And then she sees it. Half hidden in the wet sand, glistening in the stormy light. Jenny picks up the telescope and brushes off the sand. It is heavy in her grasp, solid. "Cool! Must be an antique." Jenny glances around, concerned that the owner might be there to reclaim this valuable object. There is no one. "Wait 'till the gang sees this," she beams, "And dad can use it when he takes the trippers out fishing." Jenny clasps her prize tightly and decides she needs to get it home. As she turns, a great roll of thunder booms across the dark and troubled sea. The gathered storm finally unleashes its fury.

Tales from the Tide

Feedback

A convincing historical story of people making their living from the sea, and the reality of loss. Atmospheric, well written with just enough dialogue and convincingly Norfolk. The authors knows about fishermen and their superstitions and has the confidence to move around in time. The jeopardy at the end is nice. Lovely description of "retired and toothless fishermen".

Highly Commended
Soul to the Sea
by Christie Davies

They heaved him in at the close of an unseasonably stormy day. The river churned mud from the banks in response to a rising, tempestuous tide and there had been no respite from the fitful downpours that drowned the returning greenness of Spring. Salt was in the air, it dried in white streaks along the forearms of the men out in the boats and settled on the lips of those in and around the castle, chafing and burning.

The Lord had raged, thrown eggs across the table in a fit of temper. The stormy sea stirred him as it had done so often before. His Lady, who knew his ire all too well, slipped from breakfast as he strode to the window, his flinty eyes transfixed on the roiling water, unable to stomach ceaselessly waiting for turncoats to return from France with arms.

From the tower, Agnes watched them drag him across the marshy, flat expanse that severed the castle keep from the sea. He was bent and bound, buckling under the weight of so many grappling hands. The net blew before him, tangled in his arms and hair, obscuring his vision like a veil. His skin glistened and rivulets of rain coursed along his muscles as he strained to evade burning ropes and spiteful hands.

The strange sight jolted her, gave pause to her mutinous thoughts, and she stumbled backwards from the precipice, suddenly afraid of being seen by the men below. The rough stone caught on the scratchy weave of her dress; the ramparts reluctant to yield her.

Agnes peered through the mudstone teeth at the booming arrival of the Lord and his entourage. He lifted the net and studied the creature, who shrank back with feral alacrity, clawing the net to his face as if to hide from the preening specimen before him. Agnes' stomach flipped and her heart hammered in her chest, the perpetual palpations reverberating like the skin of a war drum.

She had managed to avoid him, eyes forever downcast and never alone in the passageways since the night he had dragged her to his bedchamber as she slipped from the kitchen; an inconsequential receptacle for his wanton urges. She met the animal beneath the finery, his hot breath misted her face and his claws raked her flesh. She'd made it to the tower that night, too – stumbling with shame, her vision fogged by tears. The sea in the air stung her nostrils and his seed burnt between her thighs, like turned wine held to a wound. She'd watched the calm water lapping gently just two miles off, longed to be shrouded by its icy silk and constricted by its terminal cold. Washed clean.

The other girls looked down sheepishly as Agnes slid into the kitchen. She self-consciously smoothed the wrinkled front of her dress to stop it from pulling.

"Ah, Agnes", Cook said as a mock smile spread across her cracked lips. "We thought you'd like this task – you're to take the creature his breakfast down". She leaned over and slapped a raw fish onto a tarnished plate customarily used for the dogs.

"What creature…" Agnes began, but Cook had already returned to the fire.

"You'll see", she muttered as she stirred a hanging pot. "You'll see. Just watch yourself, Agnes". She sighed and turned back to face the girls, a cruel sneer animating her face. "Who knows what the woodwose is capable of?"

The stairs were damp, green lichen bloomed between the stones. Agnes clutched the rope to steady herself, taking care not to upend the fish. Cook's words had not frightened her as intended; after all, Agnes had seen this man and knew he was borne of the sea, not the trees. She had watched him cowed with fear, not instigating it.

There was very little light in the belly of the castle. Agnes edged forward, trailing her hand along the cold stone as she pressed toward the dungeon. The man's capture the night before played out in her mind; the net, the number of men it had taken to restrain him. She knew she should be afraid – she was about to come face to face with a beast, but she wasn't; rather, she was overcome with curiosity to see this being supposedly birthed by the waves.

Surprisingly, the door to the cell had been propped open, and there was no guard or attendant. So unusual was this that Agnes feared she had taken a wrong turn along the way. Frantic scurrying drew her forward, and she gasped at a cage of clawing rats. Agnes had heard of this particular treatment in the encouragement of prisoners.

Once in the doorway, she knew she had found her destination, for there he was – the Wildman. At the sight of her, he raised his hands to cover his face and pushed himself backwards into the corner of the cell. Agnes hadn't known what to expect, but it wasn't this – she hadn't thought to find a man so imbued with fear that a slip of a girl would drive him away whimpering in fright. Agnes knelt, and pity swelled in her heart at the bite marks pitting his torso and the crude incisions in the deviant skin between his fingers and toes. His bloodied mouth and eyes were swollen shut. She pushed the stinking fish towards him, shamed at her part in this torture. The light from a guttering candle fell across him, highlighting the muscular undulations of his statuesque body and the thick, luxuriant hair falling down his back like a curtain. She saw a man, not a beast. A man with a form that would induce envy in every lord, knight and warrior.

A new routine soon settled. Guttural groans from the dungeon gave a new backdrop to daily life within the castle walls. The people were uncomfortably aware that their Lord had taken a perverse interest in their maritime guest – low voices muttered of his lingering gaze, which now turned to the stairs that led below rather than the windows facing the sea. They whispered of how he was increasingly partial to fish straight from the water, how he downed their squeezed juices, his face painted with defiance as he slammed the tankard on the table once finished.

It was clear to all who had seen the Wildman that the poor creature was not silent through choice and that when he recoiled from the touch of the men, it was as much to do with their physical proximity as the weapons they wielded. Agnes saw fear in the man's eyes but also confusion – the absolute bewilderment akin to that of a lost child. Indeed, the unlined face and smooth skin hinted that this was a boy rushed to manhood by means beyond his awareness and control. Agnes sat by him and spoke softly of the castle and its tower, of the marsh, the river and the sea. She told of the kitchen and its smoke, the Lord and the seed he had wildly planted inside her and how it had taken root. She cried, and he watched, never inching closer or meeting her gaze.

After nigh on a month of confinement, it was decided that he should be allowed to swim – it was feared that without reunion with water, this demon fish would shrivel and waste to nothing. A vast net was constructed, and strung across the harbour to prevent his escape. Agnes had watched the men carry it down in the early hours, whilst battling the resurgent sickness that plagued her. Such fitful nights rendered her reluctant to leave her bed, and she often appeared late to the kitchen, much to Cook's dismay.

"Up today, Agnes, not down," Cook said, sighing as Agnes rushed in on the morning of the swim. She stood still, unsure what Cook meant – it was always down to the dungeon for her in the morning – she had hoped to speak to him, explain what would be happening, though she was till unsure whether he understood a word she said.

Cooked sighed at the puzzled expression on her

face, "You're to go up and serve the Lady her breakfast this morning, Agnes. She asked for you especially." Agnes nodded, dumbfounded.

Upstairs, the Lady was sweating, enormous with child. When Agnes entered the room, the Lady shifted upright and frowned. Agnes' nerves jangled with fear, and she held her hands together to still their shaking. Her mind flooded with the possibility that the Lady knew of the attention she had received – she would not care that Agnes had no say or agency in the matter.

The Lady cleared her throat loftily for attention, and when Agnes looked up, she pointed towards her cup. Agnes hastily moved for the jug. As she lifted to pour, swollen fingers encircled her wrist.

"Girl, I am not blind," the Lady hissed, pulling Agnes towards her. "I can see that you begin to swell with life".

Agnes pressed her lips together, determined not to show the terror she felt squirming inside her, a snake slowly coiling, rooting her to the spot.

"I will not have it!" the Lady whispered, the venom curdling her voice to a growl. "It has been brought to my ear that the only men you have been in proximity with are my husband and that thing that dwells beneath." At the insinuation, Agnes began to shake – so this was the Lady's plan, to spread a more convenient truth than her husband taking an unwilling serving girl to bed. Space would readily be made for her and her baby down below; they would anticipate the arrival of another wildling with great greed.

Agnes raised her eyes to the Lady but could not muster the strength to speak, for remaining upright was taking every bit of it. The Lady's eyes bored into Agnes, and Agnes held on as long as she could until the sobs surfaced. Salty tracks ran down her cheeks, like inlets in the marsh. Agnes turned and ran from the room, not caring about the consequence of such subordination – nothing could be worse than the Lady's plans to announce her coupled with the Wildman.

Agnes was soon swept up by the crowds headed for the harbour. There was a buoyant mood amongst those who resided within the castle, keen to see the Wildman temporarily returned to his habitat. As Agnes bustled through the open castle doors, carried along by the throng, she stumbled and felt the sharp pain of a loose stone cut into the palm of her hand. Kneeling on the dusty track, she watched blood trickle from her closed fist onto a large round rock. She pocketed it as she stood.

Agnes merged with the other people, the crowd swelling like a wave as they neared the port. Her pockets bulged by the time they crashed and dispersed

Soul to the Sea

along the wall and between the moored boats. Through sails snapping in the wind, Agnes saw his body meet the water and felt the calmness settle as his arching torso sliced through the surface. Minutes passed, but he did not reappear. Agnes trudged along the jetty, laden dress dragging behind her.

Cheers erupted at the Wildman floating serenely on the other side of the barrier, free. His strong arms cutting through the water were mesmerising; the arch and relief of his back, beautiful as he dove through the oncoming waves. He paused, seemingly uncertain as to whether he should return to the shouting guards. He bobbed in the swell and fall of the water for no longer than a minute and then turned and left, soul to the sea. No one saw Agnes leave, too. No one saw her step discretely from the wall and sink. The bubbles from her smiling mouth streamed up and broke the surface. A final shout, a final sigh.

Feedback

There was something familiar about this story, as if it might have been based on a piece of folklore. It was nicely written, and I especially liked the contrast between the anonymous, faceless Lord and the more real, more human Agnes. The sad inevitability of the ending was lifted by the idea of the sea as home – somewhere clean.

The Wedding of the Sea
by Michael Giddings

The ring arced through the air, a glint of gold tracing its path as it rose and descended and then fell gently into the sea. Tara pictured it continuing down and down to the bottom, nestling in the restless sand.

She turned up her collar as a gust of wind blew along the pier and she smiled at the thought that it might have been Gavin, sending his thanks and his blessing for her gesture of love and affection. She had longed so much to be reunited with him, spent so much time on pointless imaginings and fantastical plots that could never come to anything, could never bring him back. Now it was relief that she felt, as if she had set herself free from the endless circle of wishing and pining and was returning the symbol of their never-ending love to him, out there where he lay peacefully recumbent, marbled with a bloom of eternal beauty, like an effigy on a tomb.

It was a year now since the sea had taken him from her. The storm had come on quicker than they'd expected and he had slipped away in a slap of foam and a vicious, moaning swell.

"He'll turn up soon," they had said, as if he was a misplaced slipper or a key to a door that no-one ever went through. "When he was a young lad he was out there for an entire day before they found him in his dinghy with his mast down, wallowing on the spring tide like a young seal pup. He was born to it. The sea won't have him."

But it had. They found the boat but he wasn't there. The storm had battered the cabin and bent the rudder and reached over the boat in a cruel embrace and lifted him out as if he was a tiny, weightless puppy.

"We'll bring him home," they had said after that, as if he was a casualty of war or a member of a cult.

But they didn't. The sea wouldn't relinquish its hold, telling everyone who listened to its gentle susurrations that it was keeping him forever.

Tara had heard the sea's message as she stood on the pier every day, gazing out as it changed mood and colour and expression and she turned the ring, his ring that he had placed on her finger, turned it round and round to assuage the pain and the longing. It was a ritual, her homage to him and their love and it was a safeguard because she knew it would have no end. As soon as she reached what she thought was the end she realised she was simply back at where she had started and she turned the ring again.

The Wedding of the Sea

"Hi Tara," someone said, and she looked up as a young man, tousle haired and ruddy, approached.

"Sam," she said and, despite herself, she smiled as she realised that she was glad to see him. "What brings you onto the pier so early in the morning?"

"I've got an early shift signing on up at the processing plant. I'm due up there at eight but it's such a lovely day I thought I'd stretch my legs first." He hesitated. "Just having a walk too are you?"

Tara didn't want to tell him what she'd just done. It was between her and Gavin.

"Yes. I don't always sleep that well – you know."

"Of course," Sam nodded sagely. "I understand." Another hesitation. "If you ever want to talk you know –well – I'm around. A drink or – whatever..." he trailed off into embarrassed silence.

"Thanks," she said softly. "I know." She was aware of the attention he'd paid her after the accident and she knew it was an act of kindness

"Well - best be off," he said and, plunging his hands into the pockets of his jeans, he walked back towards the esplanade.

Tara turned back to the sea. She wondered if Sam had seen her throw the ring. She didn't mind. It was still personal between her and Gavin, only he would know why she had done it, what it meant.

Tales from the Tide

As she stood there she thought for the thousandth time about their wedding day. It seemed like it was only yesterday and yet it was so long ago as well. Time playing its tricks as usual. He had insisted on the church. "It's the right place to get married," he said. "One day I'll end up in the graveyard there I suppose," he added, and then laughed. "Not for another fifty years or more though."

She'd loved his laugh, his carefree way of expressing himself. It felt like nothing was beyond the two of them, nothing was impossible and she'd looked forward to their new life together.

The wedding was in mid-May and they'd gone to Italy for their honeymoon – a resort down the coast from Venice. They hadn't strayed far from the hotel and its beach. They hadn't needed to, but the hotel receptionist did suggest they go on a trip to Venice.

"*Venezia*," she gushed. "A wonder of the world and so easy on the train. Tomorrow will be a good day to go."

"Well we don't want to miss out on that, do we?" Gavin said, turning to her and smiling. "You only live once."

They set off early the next day and – yes – it was easy to get the train. They were eager to see the sights but neither of them was prepared for the sudden explosion of colour and activity as they walked out of

The Wedding of the Sea

the station. They were immediately in the centre of Venice, standing by a wide canal, and Tara thought it all looked like a giant film set. There were crowds everywhere, and they followed them slowly towards St Marks Square stopping off for a coffee and slice of pizza in a tiny cafe.

"There's so many people," Gavin said to the waiter who served them.

"Of course," he said. "Today everyone comes to Venice. It is the *Sposalizio del mare.*"

Seeing their blank look he continued. "Every year at the *Ascencione* – the Ascension Day – the mayor of Venice throws the wedding ring into the sea. It is a symbol of the marriage of Venice with the sea. It is a union that lasts forever. The sea is very important here. It is why Venice was so rich and powerful. And today," he added as he hurried away, "is the *Ascencione.*"

They followed the crowds slowly to St Marks Square where there was a huge fair, and there were scores of boats all decked out with ribbons and flags and pennants of every colour, bobbing up and down on the water. They cheered and clapped as the crews pulled at the oars, racing against each other and clipping through the water like brilliant clockwork toys on a giant pond.

"We ought to have a day like this back home," laughed Gavin as they strolled back to the station. "It'd certainly pull in the tourists – and there's several places that do pizza. Wouldn't be quite the same though would it?" He laughed again and then looked straight at her. "This is sort of special," he said and he stopped and kissed her as the crowds surged round them.

After they got home Gavin found an article about the ceremony on the internet. It was just as the waiter had said; Venice's annual marriage with the sea – the *Sposalizio* - ancient and symbolic and charged with meaning. They both remembered it and explained it all as they showed everyone the photos.

Afterwards they started their married life, and it was just as she had imagined. They'd both lived with their parents before so it was all new and she loved every minute of it. They made cakes together and bought furniture and went for walks along the beach at low tide and it was all simple and delightful and she'd never been happier.

On the last morning she got up and waved him off from the front door. It was still dark and beginning to rain and the wind was blowing the leaves down the street. He was going out alone as he did sometimes and she'd told him to be careful and he turned and said,

The Wedding of the Sea

"I'll be back soon" and blew her a kiss. It was the last time she saw him.

After it happened she'd not cried at first. She was sure he was coming back and everyone rallied round telling her it would be OK.

But gradually they all knew that it wouldn't be OK. There were kind words, well meant, but they bounced off her and she developed a hard skin, a carapace that shielded her from the pain. It wasn't the right way to be, and she had the sense that this was the calm before the storm when her emotions would envelop her, devour her piece by piece, so she fought to retain the calm, terrified of her feelings and the way that they would overwhelm her if she gave in to them. She went to the pier nearly every day, to remember him, yes, but also to look for the courage to face the storm.

Then one day she dared to look at the photos of them together and she quickly came to their honeymoon and the day in Venice. She cried then, great sobs welling up from the pool of pain deep inside her, but gradually she started to feel that there was a way out, a way to quieten her anguish and achieve some sort of resolution. The day in Venice had been special, just as he said, the best day of the honeymoon, which in turn had been the best days of their short married life. Now the two of them would have another wedding, a wedding of the sea, and his ring that he had given her as a symbol of his love would be with him, and the sea would join them together again and she would grieve and regret but it would also give her the courage to go on.

After she had thrown the ring into the sea, like a renewal of her vows, she went down to the pier less often, but when she did go she began to notice again everything that was there– boats returning with the catch of the day or loaded with day trippers out on a spree, gulls wheeling and calling on the breezes that ruffled the waves and children licking and slurping ice creams bought for them by indulgent grandparents.

And several times she saw Sam as he went to or from work. They exchanged a few words, and he always asked how she was. Then one day a few months after she'd consigned her ring to the sea, she saw him coming towards her as she came off the pier. She smiled as she recognised his lumbering gait and his broad grin and she heard Gavin telling her that it was alright and now was the time, so that when Sam asked her how she was she replied: "I'm doing fine now Sam – and by the way, is the offer of a drink still open?"

He beamed back, "Of course it is, anytime."

"OK," she said. "How about this weekend?"

The Wedding of the Sea

Feedback

A very good story. A drowned sailor, but a hopeful ending. The characters, despite being briefly described, are convincing and three dimensional, and the holiday flashback with its detail and humanity, is well written. I enjoyed the characters and the setting, and could easily imagine the spectacle of the Sea Wedding in Venice.

Author Biographies

Iain Andrews

A Glaswegian by birth, Iain has lived in East Anglia for most of his life, and can be witnessed playing walking football or singing self-penned nonsensical ditties at the Norwich Folk Club, an activity which allows him to dispense with all accepted forms of grammar (and good taste).

His full-length whodunnit *Rosary Road*, written under his pen name of Robert Chandler, is published by Hobart Books. He's also self-published a supernatural mystery called *A Conspiracy of Ravens*.

Jana Bakunina

Jana Bakunina is a Russian-born Londoner. She writes about Russia, London and everything in between, especially if it involves identity or a lost sense of belonging.

She is the author of a memoir, Bird's Milk (2017) about growing up in the Soviet Union and moving to the West. Jana has written for the Financial Times and New Statesman, and she is a regular guest speaker at Dalkey Book Festival in Ireland. Her stories were longlisted for the 2021 and 2022 Fish Short Story Prize, shortlisted for the 2022 Bridport Prize, and she became the finalist of the 2022 London Independent Short Story Prize.

Helen Bromovsky

Helen Bromovsky is based in Somerset.

Helen originally studied French and German literature followed by a degree course in Creative Writing and Critical Reading.

Mesmerised by an ocean of writers, a lot of travel and a fascination with the diversity of cultures and the developing world and after ten years of involvement with marine conservation and the trials and tribulations of life a collection of short stories emerged, of which, Albert is one.

Helen is a founder member of The Mediterranean Conservation Foundation based in the eastern Mediterranean and an enthusiastic supporter of solution-based conservation and grass roots education. After many years as a designer and creative director of The Ottoman Collection inspired by ancient indigenous designs the vessel for creative expression has metamorphosed into awareness using words and storytelling.

Tales from the Tide

T M Davids

T M Davids has always been a 'scribbler.' From 12 years old she has been drawn to the written word and the power it possesses.

Although life took her on many different paths, she has always immersed herself in creative writing through a variety of workshops, both local and academic, and earning an Undergraduate Diploma in Creative Writing at Oxford University Department for Continuing Education.

She was awarded the 'Investment for Individuals Award' from Southern Arts to help with the first edit of her novel, which she is refining at present.

As a qualified Psychotherapist, a new layer was added to her writing – playing with narrative writing as a therapeutic tool, changing traumatic stories we hold for ourselves to find release and sanctuary with a new perspective, creative storytelling, and ultimately, release.

Her greatest passion is unlocking voices and playing with reality, testing the boundaries of what we can discover about ourselves and our world using magical realism and fairytale.

Author Biographies

Christie Davies

Christie enjoys reading and writing Sci-Fi and is currently working on a Young Adult project in this genre. She joined the NWC in 2020 and has since won the Members' shield for the Olga Sinclair competition and has been shortlisted in the main competition twice. Recently she has been a finalist and received honourable mentions in various Globe Soup story writing competitions.

Mary Ellen Fox

After leaving a short-lived rock and roll career in accountancy, Mary decided to start a course in creative writing at City Lit in Holborn, London. Here she was encouraged to write short stories. She has since been long and short-listed in numerous competitions in both the UK and US. Her stories have been published in many UK anthologies including the Fish anthology, the GRIST anthology of protest, the Momaya Short Story Review, The Loop anthology by Michael Terence Publishing and the Henshaw 5 anthology. In the US her stories have appeared in the Indignor House anthology, Stories through the Ages Babyboomers and the Saints and Sinners LGBTQ literary festival anthology. She currently resides in Epsom with her husband, two children and a pair of hens named Tikka and Jalfrezi.

Michael Giddings

After a career in the City of London, Michael moved to Norfolk to pursue his passions for gardening and writing. He's written a self-published memoir about his experiences in Spain in the final years of General Franco's rule and also a novel for which he's seeking an agent or publisher. He's also written several prize winning short stories and is currently working on another full length novel.

He writes widely from his life experience, but also approaches subjects from a viewpoint that attempts to explore not only his own view but also the imagined experience of a diverse cast of characters. He finds this wide ranging process very effective in the creative act of writing fiction and it leads to a more complete picture of whatever he's trying to depict.

Themes that emerge most frequently in his writing include: coming of age, the effects of time and its passing, the difficulty in interpreting someone's inner thoughts from their outward actions and the challenge of finding feeling, meaning and identity in the 21st century.

Author Biographies

Amongst the main influences on his writing are: F. Scott Fitzgerald, Andre Aciman, Ford Madox Ford, Andre Gide, William Boyd, Anne Tyler, John Irving and a number of modern South American writers.

Natalie Hart

Natalie Hart lives in Birmingham but spends as much time as possible in a fishing village in the Scottish Highlands. Her family's connection to the village goes back for as long as anyone can remember and was the inspiration for her short story *Fish Guts*.

Natalie is a graduate of two Faber writing courses and is currently writing her debut novel *The Cuckoos of Nightingale Ward*. The story, inspired by her experience being an inpatient on an eating disorder ward, follows a woman in her twenties as she grapples with a tenacious illness. It explores the relationships she forms with the other patients and is at its heart a story of friendship and belonging.

Natalie has worked with young people in theatre for twenty years which has kept her creative juices flowing on a daily basis. This led her to completing a PhD at The University of Warwick which examines the impact of class and ethnicity on engagement with Birmingham Repertory Theatre's Youth Theatre.

Natalie is neurodivergent which she believes bring a unique quality to her world view and writing.

Samantha Mattocks

Samantha Mattocks is a Norfolk-based award-winning writer and journalist, photographer, magazine publisher, and foodie.

She's been writing all her life, from creating stories telling of mythical lands and writing plays and poetry when she was a child to writing short stories, novellas, a novel, a children's book series, and much more.

In 2004, Samantha founded The Arabian Magazine, all about Arabian horses, and with that she travelled the world. That inspired her first full-length novel, *Sandstorm*, published during lockdown.

Her time with The Arabian Magazine also inspired her to collate her poetry/photography collection, *progress*, published in 2009. The poetry was from her late teens/early 20s, married with photographs she'd taken around the world on her travels.

In October 2023, Samantha launched her first children's book, *Mister Mishkins' Apothecary,* the same night she learned she'd won the Norwich Writers Members Shield.

Both *Sandstorm* – now re-published under her penname Adelaide Halsey – and *Mister Mishkins'* are the first books in their respective series, with sequels already well underway.

Samantha also owns The Delicate Diner, a foodie website that led her to compete in MasterChef 2019 and then becoming the food and drink columnist for Norfolk Online. During lockdown, she published a series of acclaimed interviews with key figures in the Norfolk foodie scene. In 2021, she co-founded *Nourish* magazine, a local food and drink magazine that ran for two years.

Samantha loves nothing more than sitting down to a blank page and how the magic happens as one begins to write, and how one creates worlds for others to lose themselves in.

You can find out more at:
www.samanthamattocks.com

Helen Murray
Helen is a history graduate with over two decades of experience working for the Norfolk Museums Service. During the covid lockdowns of 2020-21, Helen researched and published a non fiction history about a house in Cromer called Newhaven Court. The project combined her lifelong passions for writing, local history and family history. She lives in Norwich with her husband and three children and is currently

working on her second book, which will centre on an artist that came to Cromer in the late Victorian period.

Fran Pridham

Fran Pridham has an MA in Creative Writing and has taught Creative Writing for many years. Her poetry has appeared in a variety of poetry magazines and anthologies. She is a Teacher Trailblazer for The Poetry Society and some of her resources have appeared on the Poetry Society Website. She has also published a poetry pamphlet Red Jam (Crocus) and the textbook The Language of Conversation (Routledge). Experimenting now with prose, her flash fiction Take the Biscuit was shortlisted in The Weaver Words Flash Competition. She loves her family, the sea, and enjoys eating almost everything except tomato ketchup.

Charlie Robinson

Charlie Robinson has lived in Beverley in the East Riding of Yorkshire for the past six years. He has worked in many industries and travelled extensively as a young man. Writing a novel was always an ambition. He published his first book in December 2022, The Siege of Mr Khan's Curry Shop. There is a sequel underway, and a finished book being edited. He has published a short story in the Best of British magazine.

R. D. Stevens

R. D. Stevens grew up in Kent, England, with an overactive imagination and a love of big questions. He is the author of two award-winning YA/NA novels - 'The Journal' (Vulpine Press, '22) and 'The Freeze' (Vulpine Press, '23) - as well as a number of short stories which have found homes with various publishers, including Reverie Magazine, Erro Press and Carrion Press.

Outside of writing, he loves to read books, play the guitar, and talk about existentialism (with anyone who'll listen). He hosts a podcast called 'Perspectives on Pages' with fellow author Benjamin Roesch, reviews indie books for notforvanity.com, and is currently working on his third novel.

Zelda C. Thorne

Zelda C. Thorne is a British writer. Her stories have been published by *Off Topic* and *The Ulu Review* as well as being featured on several podcasts including *Tall Tale TV*. She was a finalist in NYC Midnight's micro-fiction competition 2023 and has several shortlisted stories on Reedsy Prompts. She grew up in Essex and now lives in Norfolk with her family. Find out more at www.zeldacthorne.com.

A Tribute to Olga Sinclair
By Anne Funnell

Olga Sinclair passed away on April 28th, 2014, aged 91.

She left us a surprise legacy in her will. This donation to our funds has supported our annual Open Prose Competition ever since. For the benefit of those reading this anthology who may not know anything about her, I have been asked to write an introduction.

Olga joined the Norwich Writers' Circle in 1960, aged 37. Within seven years, she had published her first book for children with Blackwell's, followed by 4 others. She published 25 books altogether under the names of Ellen Clare, Olga Daniels, and her married name of Olga Sinclair, with several other publishers, depending on the genre. She wrote romantic historical fiction sticking as far as possible to the facts, which she meticulously researched. I remember her telling me of a visit to Scotland, and the book she wrote afterwards called, *Gretna Green* (A romantic History). The last book she wrote was called *The Countess and the Miner*, published in 2005 by Robert Hale.

Tales from the Tide

For Poppyland she wrote two historical books, *When Wherries Sailed By* (1987) and *Potter Heigham (The Heart of Broadland)* (1989).

She acted as Magistrate for several years, giving her an understanding of current affairs and local issues.

In 1968 she became a committee member for the Circle, and she was the Hon Treasurer for a couple of years. She became Vice-President in 1980. After Mary Ingate died in 1991, she was elected as President in 1992. She remained a loyal and hard-working member, graciously handing over the trophies at our annual prize-givings, until the AGM of July 2012, after which she felt unable to continue.

She was a member of the Romantic Novelists Association, and encouraged me to attend meetings in London, and we went together to conferences which took place in University buildings during the summer vacations from 1992 to 2005.

We had more than one garden party at their Dove House Farm in Potter Heigham. Her husband, Stanley, who sadly predeceased her, had a very quirky sense of humour for a headmaster of Thorpe School, Norwich. He organised one quiz where we had to identify monstrous or down-right odd "ornaments" he had carved and constructed in his garden. One I remember was a yellow "Marigold", which was a rubber washing-up-glove suddenly rising up out of the pond on a pneumatic blast set off by a time-switch.

Olga enjoyed country dancing, and when widowed attended dances with her dancing partner and chauffeur, Charles. Her friends from the group attended her funeral and afterwards performed dances for us, thus making this the jolliest funeral I have ever attended.

Olga embodied in her warmth and humour the aim of the founding members of the Circle, in 1943, "To encourage the art and craft of writing and promote good fellowship amongst Norfolk and Norwich writers generally."

About the Norwich Writers' Circle

In 1943, at the height of World War 2, a small group of enthusiastic creative writers, both amateur and professional, joined together and established Norwich Writers' Circle. The aim of the founders was to "encourage the art and craft of writing and promote good fellowship amongst Norwich and Norfolk writers generally.

The aim remains unchanged, and it is in that spirit that our Circle continues to flourish today, with members work representative of a number of diverse literary styles and genres.

Over the years we have welcomed writers such as Louise de Bernieres, D.J. Taylor, Kathryn Hughes, Simon Scarrow, George Szirtes, Rachel Hore, Patrick Barkham, Alison Bruce, Hayley Long, Heidi Williamson, Keiron Pim, Elly Griffiths and Emma Healey.

We host talks, workshops and manuscript evenings. Each season we offer opportunities for members and guests to enter in-house competitions, each judged by professional authors, with trophies awarded to our most successful writers.

Two years ago, we launched a new membership type—Online Membership—which opens up talks and workshops to people around the globe. In addition to this, we hold a summer programme on various aspects of writing.

And finally, we are proud of our annual Olga Sinclair Prize Competition (formerly the Olga Sinclair Open Prose Competition), with themes drawn from Norwich life, now in its eighth year, offering generous cash prizes to winning entrants. In addition, members of the NWC have the opportunity for their entries adjudicated for the much-coveted Anne Funnell Challenge Shield.

For more information, please see our website at www.norwichwriters.com

Or at facebook.com/Norwich Writers

Or email an enquiry to: queries@norwichwriters.com

Printed in Great Britain
by Amazon